THE KIDNAPPING OF TAMMY FITZGERALD

SECOND EDITION

THE KIDNAPPING OF TAMMY FITZGERALD

SECOND EDITION

TIGHE TAYLOR

ReadersMagnet, LLC.

TABLE OF CONTENTS

Other Books by Tighe Taylor

The Tragic Death of Marina Habe
The Kidnapping of Taylor Shaw
The Kidnapping of Isabel Miller

Always bear in mind that
Your own resolution to succeed
Is more important
Than any one thing.

Abraham Lincoln

Five Years Ago

It was 5:30 in the afternoon in the California desert. In winter, the days are short. Night would be falling soon. In the dim light of dusk, the outline of the farm house and barn situated on the property were barely visible. Though known for its temperate climate, the forecast was for a considerable rain storm to be accompanied by thunder and lightning.

My name is Taylor Shaw. I live on this property with my mother. Though only 14 years old, due to the fact that my father left us when I was 10 and because my mother is a raging alcoholic unable to take care of herself, I was left in charge of our meager enterprise.

My mother was bitter, but her bitterness would become more intense as time went on. She always treated me as if I was nothing - not pretty enough, not smart enough, not accomplished enough. I guess she felt that she had to keep me down to make her feel better about herself and to keep me chained to this farm, as it was her only means of support. Without me working the farm, she was certain that she would perish, which is not far from the truth.

We had a few animals, but the main business was oranges. Earlier, I coaxed the animals (mainly chickens and goats) into the barn, to get them out of the rain, the threat of which was fast becoming a reality.

I took Molly, my horse, out to ride around the orchard to make sure everything was in order, as best it could be.

A light rain had started, but the sky was becoming seriously black, indicating that much more was to come. I walked Molly back into the barn and into her stall, gave her a rub down, and headed across the yard, the short distance from the barn to the house, on foot.

Lighting lit the sky sufficiently to see the outline of the barn and our small house and yard.

I saw a large black pick-up truck with six headlights parked in front of the house. This meant that my mother was entertaining one of her "friends," most of whom she met at the local bar.

This was never a good thing. Invariably, she and her friends would get drunk. My greatest fear was that one of them would lose interest in her and start after me. Even though I was only 14, I was beginning to look old enough to be mistaken as a little older. My mother, even though not terribly old, was a mess from drinking and doing nothing productive all day long for many years.

My plan was to sneak into the house and into my bedroom. This was difficult as the front door opened into the living room, which was small, and was where my mother was entertaining her friend.

The rain was now coming down in buckets, and I could not stay outside any longer. I entered the house and moved past my mother and her guest. I made it to my bedroom, but I would have to cross back through the living room to get to the bathroom. During this crossing, I would certainly be noticed.

I made it to my bedroom, but while crossing the living room to reach the bathroom, my mother's friend reached out to grab me. He addressed me in a demeaning tone saying, "Who do we have here?" I guess he felt that his tone should match my low opinion of myself.

My mother responded, "Please leave her alone. She is just a child."

He replied, "She doesn't look like no child to me."

He grabbed for me and said in a loud voice, "Come here. Let's have a look at you."

I eluded him and entered the bathroom and immediately locked the door.

He tried to enter. When he found that the door was locked, he became agitated and yelled at my mother, "Get this door open right now."

My mother replied that she did not have a key. He slapped her across the face and began trying to break the door down.

While all of this was going on, I made my way out of the bathroom window and into the back yard.

As lightning bolted across the sky, I was reminded not only of this night but of all of the horrible nights that I experienced with my mother over the years.

I doubted that the relationship between us would ever be filled with anything positive. I reconciled myself to the possibility that this was all that I deserved. I would just have to soldier on and see if we could ever connect the space between us.

With all of these fears swirling around in my head, after exiting the window, I fell to the ground where I became covered in mud. I did not care. With no time to think, I took off running, mud and all, across the orchard to our neighbor's house. Heavy rain and lightning continued as I ran. I was soaked as I weaved through the orange trees.

Inside of our house, my mother's friend finally broke the door down. He immediately saw that I was not there and that I must have left through the window which was still ajar.

He became enraged. He yelled at my mother, "Where is she going?"

My mother replied, "She's in the orchard now. You will never catch her. Besides she's nothing. You can do much better."

He yelled, "There is only one other farm in these parts. The one where the old lady lives. I'll just go there and take her from the old coot."

He pushed my mother down on the couch, got into his truck, and headed to the neighboring farm. The neighboring farm was occupied by an elderly lady by the name of Nettie. A truly wonderful person like so many of the women who worked these farms after their husbands passed away.

I reached Nettie's front door which was under the cover of the overhanging roof.

I said to Nettie, "I'm sorry to bother you, but one of my mother's friends began to get physical with me, and I had to sneak out the bathroom window. I'm afraid that he might come here."

Nettie said to me sternly, "You did the right thing. Go back to the kitchen and call the sheriff. Then stay in the kitchen and do not come out unless I tell you to."

Finding no reason to argue, I did as she asked. Unknown to me, Nettie took her Remington out of the gun cabinet and loaded it and waited.

A little while later, the black truck pulled up in front of Nettie's front door. The rain began to subside to a light drizzle.

My mother's friend exited the truck and headed towards the house.

Nettie opened the front door and stood, with her rifle, on the porch. The man stated, "I've come for the girl. Give her to me now."

With resolve in her voice, Nettie replied, "If you want to take her, you will have to do it over the dead body of one of us."

Not believing that she would shoot, the man advanced towards the porch. He was now clearly on Nettie's property.

Nettie leveled the rifle and shot him on the side of his left boot. He was startled. He stopped to examine his foot. It appeared as if only his boot was hit.

After looking at his foot for a few minutes, the sheriff arrived and came towards the man from behind. The sheriff said, "I heard that you have come here to take Mrs. Shaw's daughter with you. Is that true?"

The man did not deny the statement but complained, "This crazy old lady shot me in the foot. I want to press charges against her."

The sheriff replied, "Nettie here is one of the best shots in the county. If she wanted to shoot you, you would be long dead or bleeding as she can shoot a fly off of an orange at 20 paces. So, we are going to consider you lucky tonight. No one comes after a child in my jurisdiction, and I mean no one. I could easily have allowed Nettie to take you out with her next shot, and not one person in these parts would complain.

"You may be from the city or some other place, but out here children are protected by the grown men and women who live here, and I include myself in that number.

"So, you have two choices. You can come with me to the station and swear out a complaint. It is almost certain that the prosecutor will not prosecute, and even if he does, no jury will convict an elderly woman who was protecting a child from a predator. Or you can leave now and never return to Newton again. Take your pick."

The man got in his truck and left town, never to be heard from again.

Nettie and Taylor thanked the sheriff, and the sheriff returned to town. Taylor returned home, unharmed, except for a little mud. She received a tongue lashing from her mother for interfering with her date, even a date with a creep like this guy. Her mother again reminded her that she was good for nothing. She couldn't even stay out of the way.

Two Years Ago

As time went by, things did not get much better with my mother. She kept me down to keep me running the farm.

I was now 16, and because of my duties, I was becoming almost an adult, at least in my mind. Also, as a 16-year old, I was beginning to look more like an adult at five foot seven and nearly 110 pounds.

I was now able to drive, which was a good thing. I drove our old green pick-up truck which allowed me to bring some of the oranges to the central market myself and enabled me to pick up laborers, tools, and supplies to keep the farm going.

One day I headed out in the truck with a load of oranges. I drove down the road and under the semi-circular sign which indicates the entrance to the central produce market where we go to sell our oranges.

Once under the sign, one could see a large, flat dirt parking area, a loading dock next to the storage building, and the main building which, in addition to the produce buyers, housed a small hardware store and a food service stand. Outside of the food service area, there were picnic tables for those who ordered food. This area was on the far side of the property and could be accessed either from the front of the main building or from the road.

I unloaded the oranges and decided to grab a sandwich. While at the food service window, I ran into Frank Diaz, one of my few friends.

Frank and I had become friends a while back. Though Latin, similar to many of the pickers, unlike the other pickers, his parents had a small farm near my mom's. Though very good looking, there was nothing romantically going on between us. I enjoyed him and had a nice time talking with him, but I was painfully shy and distrusting of men and never had any kind of relationship with someone of the opposite sex.

Frank just turned 18 and was about to graduate from high school, and I was only 16, making a physical relationship technically illegal in California. I was a sophomore at the same school, Newton High School, where he was a senior.

Both of our farms, the market, and the high school were located in Newton, a lower-class farming town. The nearest town to Newton was Haven. Haven was a more upwardly mobile place with a budding middle class and even a small upper-middle class.

For years, Newton was isolated from Haven because the road between the two towns ran through a dangerous mountain pass.

As time progressed, however, a new interstate highway was constructed which would make the trip from Haven to Newton an easy one. Also, a new upper middle-class subdivision known as Haven Lakes was built along this new interstate.

Rumors swirled about how the interstate and the subdivision were built. The front person for both projects was a man by the name of Don Fitzgerald. According to my mother, who went to high school with him, he was a star football player.

However, he was injured in his last game and was unable to go onto college and the pros. He became a real estate operator. Some say he had the wherewithal to build the interstate and the subdivision projects while others maintained that he must have had a backer.

The interstate did greatly improve the prospects for those of us in Newton.

Frank and I each bought a sandwich and headed for a table on the perimeter of the property. We sat. The conversation became oddly serious, at least by my estimation. Frank told me that he would be leaving Newton after high school to enter the police department which was located in Haven. This was not news to me, as his wish to go into the police department was the subject of conversations before this one. However, as his graduation was approaching, he had become more serious about it.

The implication was that we would not be able to continue whatever relationship it was he thought we had. I was fine with it as I never thought that we had a relationship anyway. Maybe Frank felt differently. But it didn't matter. He would be leaving, and, as his friend, it was my job to support him and his decision, which actually made it easier for me.

I thanked him for our talk. Looking back, I can see why he might have been a little confused. We spent many hours talking about our lives and his plans for the future. I was so young that I did not really have plans to share, so sharing was not important to me. But I was a willing listener which he might have confused for interest. I still had a great deal to learn about the opposite sex.

Later, I would take on a babysitting assignment for the Fitzgerald family first in Haven and then at their new home in the newly built subdivision of Haven Lakes. I was to look after their daughter Tammy who was at an age where she needed guidance from her mother. Unfortunately, her mother was too busy with her new civic duties as the wife of a major real estate developer.

Frank went back to his family farm. I presume that he was feeling as if he had been fair with me, which he certainly was, or would have been if we actually had a relationship.

I collected the paper plates and cups and began to throw the assorted paper products and left-over food into the trash.

Over my shoulder, I saw a very expensive Mercedes Benz convertible stop. It appears as if it had accessed the area directly from the road. The car pulled along the last row of tables and stopped.

Four rich white kids exited the car. They were dressed in preppy attire, very different from the usual customers who were in jeans and work clothes. It was now about four o'clock, and the patrons were long gone. I was virtually by myself.

The four boys came over to me.

They were generally rude. They asked why I was dressed like a farm worker, if I went to school, and whether I would be interested in a date with one or more of them.

I tried my best to explain to them that I was dressed like a farm worker because I was a farm worker, that I went to Newton High School, and that I was not interested in a date with any one of them.

This displeased them, and all four approached me in an aggressive manner. As they approached, the one who appeared to be their leader drew out an 8-inch hunting knife. A question passed through my mind: Did this boy know how to use such a knife? If used improperly, it could leave you with a nasty scar on your dominant hand. At that point, I figured that I was in for a fight against the four of them.

Fortunately for me (or them), a group of five or six pickers who just finished up in the fields was dropped off from an open truck by the tables to wait for their ride home.

Sensing that I might be in a little trouble, they came over to me and my new "friends". The lead picker asked me if I was alright. I said that I was because I knew that if I said differently these four clowns would get the beat down of their lives, that is, if they made it out alive.

All of the pickers had their machetes that they had been using in the field as well as other assorted knives.

The lead picker, a nice-looking man about 35, said to the boys, "You boys might want to leave her alone. I've seen her work in the fields, and I can tell you in no uncertain terms that she works as hard as any four men. Plus, I plan on lending her my 18-inch machete to even things up as there are four of you and you have a knife, though a small one. Your best bet would be to get back into your car and leave. She just might be a little more trouble than you need right now."

Without another word, the boys returned to their car and left the market. The pickers left with their ride. I left in my truck.

I returned home to the farm. My mother asked why I was so late. I told her that I ran into Frank and lost track of time. My mother said that she really wished that I could meet a nice normal young man implying that Frank and the other pickers were beneath me.

I didn't have time to argue. I told her that she had nothing to worry about. I had no relationship with Frank, and, besides, he would be leaving for the police academy soon.

All I could think about was just how completely and utterly wrong my mother was in her assessment of Frank and the pickers, which happens when you base your opinions on stereotypes rather than getting to know people.

A while later, the little girl for whom I babysat, Tammy Fitzgerald, was kidnapped. The police were unable to find her. Her case became closed, and she was considered legally dead, funeral and all. I would try to muster my own investigation, but my efforts were dismissed as juvenile by law enforcement.

This left me with no place to turn. Having run out of options, I decided to enroll in school. I enrolled at Newton Junior College. My first day of class had arrived.

CHAPTER 1

Newton Junior College, Constitution 101– First Day of Class

"The United States Constitution freed no slaves, gave no women the right to vote, and provided no services to the poor, or to anyone else for that matter.

"Hello everyone, my name is Professor Richard Miller. This class is Constitution 101.

"If you're interested, I am an attorney. After law school, I worked for the District Attorney's office in Haven for four years, until I was 28. That year I found out that my mother was ill. Because my father had already passed, I moved to my mother's house in Newton to take care of her.

"Shortly after moving back, my mother also passed. As I already signed a two-year contract, I decided to stay on to fulfil my commitment. When that is up, I plan on returning to my old job in Haven.

"As an Assistant District Attorney, much of my work involved criminal law. I worked with the professional investigators in the DA's office and the various forensic experts available to us.

"Enough about me, we may as well get started with the subject matter. The original Constitution, the original document without its amendments, consisted of only seven fairly short articles. Since 1789, there have been 27 Amendments, including the first ten Amendments known as the Bill of Rights.

"The first three articles deal with the three different branches of government. Article IV deals with the relationship between the States and the federal government. Article V deals with the process of amendment.

"Article VI provides that the debts of the States shall be valid against the United States, that the laws of the United States shall be the supreme law of the land, and that there will be no religious test to hold office. Article VII provides that only nine States would be necessary to ratify the Constitution.

"Article III provides that the judicial power of the United States shall be vested in one supreme court and such other inferior courts as Congress may establish.

"Does anyone have an idea as to what is one of the most important things that the Supreme Court does?"

A young lady raises her hand.

"Yes, and may I know your name?"

"Taylor Shaw."

"And what do you think?"

"I think that one of the most important things that the Supreme Court does is to declare certain acts of Congress and executive orders unconstitutional."

"Do you know what this is called?"

"Yes. It is called judicial review."

"Very good. And did you know that nowhere in the Constitution is the Supreme Court granted the power of judicial review. The Supreme Court did not have this power until 1803, 16 years later, when it gave that power to itself in the case of Marbury vs Madison."

It was time for class to end.

"Everyone, please read Chapters 1 through 3 in you textbook, and I will see you at our next meeting."

All of the 30 or so students began to file out of the classroom and into the hall. Taylor Shaw lingered a bit but soon also left.

CHAPTER 2

Taylor Shaw

The student who answered the question about the Supreme Court, Taylor Shaw, stood out. Yes, she was beautiful and seemingly intelligent, but other than that, she seemed a little older and more mature.

I would come to find out later that she was a year or two older than most of her classmates. She stayed out of school for a year due to her connection to a crime committed in the community. She also had work duties in her family business, and she helped her friend Moose, his wife Carol, and some of their friends with their businesses.

Her approach was different than the other girls. Though she looked roughly the same, she did not appear to be interested in participating in the typical high school activities which captivated the others.

She did not appear to have any friends, male or female, in class. She did not appear to be put off by her classmates; she just seemed uninterested in their interests. Their lack of interest in her appeared about the same.

She was kind of a loner. That high school social outcast thing, even though she was technically in college.

She intrigued me so thoroughly that I could only hope that I could get through the semester with as little contact with her as possible, to keep from making a total fool of myself with a girl

10 years my junior. I would never let on. I would just ignore her, teach my class, and go back to my work in Haven.

Not much chance of this happening you say? Unbeknownst to me at the time, you would have been right.

Junior college is an interesting concept. It is a place halfway between high school and college. The students want to continue in the social structure of high school which is familiar and comfortable and affords them protection from the real world. Also, in high school one does not have to be a self-starter, as is necessary for success in a four-year college.

In my four-year college and three-year law school experience, a teacher would assign reading and say, 'ok, go learn.' A junior college student is not quite ready for that.

From a geographical standpoint, this part of the world is somewhat defined by the two towns that are roughly adjacent to one another, Newton, the town in which the junior college is located, and Haven, the larger town over the hill.

For many years, before the interstate highway was completed, the only way to reach Newton was through a narrow and dangerous mountain pass road.

Its inaccessibility, and the fact that it was a farming town in which nothing intellectually stimulating took place made Newton pretty low on the social ladder. Haven, on the other hand, was a commercial center, easily accessible to most of the State.

While Newton's population consisted of lower-class farmers with small farms, Haven was developing a growing upper middle class of white-collar workers, including lawyers, accountants, real estate developers, and the business people who sold the raw materials obtained from Newton and places such as Newton.

Several months ago, a relatively expensive subdivision was built in the foothills between Haven and Newton known as Haven Lakes. As local lore went, to facilitate the development of Haven Lakes, it became necessary to complete the interstate highway between Haven and Newton. It was thought that as a side benefit, the prospects of Newton would improve.

Taylor Shaw lived with her mother on their family farm in Newton. Her father walked out on them when Taylor was only 10. This left Taylor's mother to run the farm, which she was not capable of doing.

Taylor had to learn the farming business literally from the ground up and ultimately became its primary operator, as her mother became a full-blown alcoholic and entertainer of unsavory men.

Taylor's mother was totally uninterested in the farming business. The remnants of the Shaw family were lower middle class and experienced few luxuries.

Before we get too far ahead of ourselves, something about Taylor seems appropriate to mention. Even though she had no father, even though her mother was an alcoholic, even though her mother berated her and tried to keep her down whenever she could, and even though she was a kid with adult responsibilities, she was not a complainer and was intensely loyal to friends and family. Two great qualities. How these qualities came into her possession, I did not know then, but I would learn as time went on.

I was born in Bryan. Bryan was a big, bustling city for this part of the world. It was also the county seat.

Each seeking to have his or her own business, my parents moved from Bryan to Haven. My mother was a doctor. She set up her own family practice. Her practice thrived.

My father was a lawyer. He established his own general practice. His practice did very well, mostly through his hard work and long hours.

Together, my parents were as close to upper middle class as you could be in Haven. They sent me off to college and then law school. I graduated from Haven State and the nearby Sutter Hall Law School when I was 24. I went to work for the DA in Haven where I planned to work and learn until I could be of some value to my father's practice.

About the time I started with the DA, my father's health began to fade. He decided that he wanted a simple life, so he sold our family house and his law practice and bought a small farm in Newton, not really knowing much about farming or about Newton.

My mother reluctantly went with him, of course. She decided to retire from her medical practice, much to the disappointment of her patients, all of whom loved her.

She possessed an ability possessed by few, the ability to listen. Many of her patients depended on her not just for medical treatment but also for all other types of support and advice, which she gave freely. That was her way.

Four years after moving to Newton, my father passed. Gradually, my mother became unable to take care of herself and certainly could not take care of a farm, even a small one. After graduation and four years working in the DA's Office, at 28, I moved to Newton to take care of her. I moved in with my mother on the farm and landed the teaching job at Newton Junior College that same year.

Shortly after my coming home, my mother passed, leaving me with a two-year contract to teach junior college. This Constitutional Law class is the last class I need to teach to finish out my teaching commitment. I am now 29.

Since the interstate was complete, some of the students from Haven could enroll in junior college in Newton. Before the interstate, it was considered geographically undesirable.

They might make this move if they could not qualify for a four-year college or if they were just not interested in taking on the presumed difficulties of such an institution. The next closest Junior College to Haven was 400 miles away.

Prior to the completion of the interstate, Newton JC was a simple place with a small, rural student body. Auto shop and agricultural classes were about all it had to offer. With the influx of students from Haven, the curriculum needed to be expanded to include more liberal arts classes, such as the one I was teaching. Speaking of teaching, the second day of class was coming up.

CHAPTER 3

Second Day of Class

"As I hope you remember from our last class, Article III covers the judiciary. Today, we will take up Articles II and I, the Presidency and the Legislature, respectively."

I went over how Article II provides for the President's election by the Electoral College, makes him the Commander in Chief, and imposes on the him the duty to give the State of the Union address.

Article II gives the President the power to grant pardons, to make treaties, and the to nominate Supreme Court Justices.

I explained that to understand how limited the office of the President was in the eyes of the founders, one might consider that with respect to the President's three powers, that is, pardon, treaties, and Supreme Court appointments, only the power to pardon could be exercised without the advice and consent of the Senate. Treaties and Supreme Court appointments required Senate approval.

I went on to compare the President's powers to the several unfettered powers of the legislature set forth in Article I. The legislature was granted the power to impose taxes, to collect duties, to borrow money, to regulate commerce, to coin money, and to declare war. The President had veto power, but a veto could be overridden by Congress.

Class ended. Students began filing out of the room.

Taylor Shaw lingered near my desk. Though all of the other students left the room and entered the hall, she remained in the classroom. I was a little apprehensive.

She spoke: "Professor Miller, is there a way that I could see you away from school?"

"Firstly, very sorry, could I get your name again?" (Brother was I a bad actor. I truly hope that I never have to quit my day job.)

"Yes. Taylor Shaw."

"Well, Ms. Shaw, I maintain regular office hours on Mondays and Wednesdays in Strom Tower. Would that work for you?"

"No, not exactly," she replied.

She continued, "I was thinking about a place a little more private and much further away from campus. I have a very delicate and private matter to discuss, and I don't want anyone to see us together."

I replied, "Under those circumstances, I would need to know a little more about the nature of the matter?"

She started, "It involves a crime which occurred a while ago. The crime was not solved, and I am looking for help solving it."

"Why me? Why not the authorities?" I replied.

"Well I heard that although you are a lawyer, much of your work was with the DA's office and its investigators. I need that kind of help."

"It is true that I was a lawyer in the District Attorney's office where I prosecuted criminals, but my contact with the investigatory branch was pretty indirect. I think local law enforcement might be a better fit for you."

She said, "Well, they tried to investigate but were unable to do anything. It was quite frustrating."

I replied, "Who is the victim?"

"Her name is Tammy Fitzgerald. She was only 12 years old when she was kidnapped from her parents' home. She was never found. After some time, the case went cold."

"How are you connected with her?"

"I was her babysitter. I know that there is more to her kidnapping than its present cold case status."

"Let me check it out, and I'll let you know," I replied.

"Ok."

"I'll see you after the next class."

She left. I went home. I checked for Tammy Fitzgerald on line. There were several stories about her and the crime, including speculation about suspects and evidence. I decided that I might just take that meeting with Ms. Shaw, now that my curiosity had been piqued.

Also, from a purely selfish standpoint, my involvement with the case would allow me to meet her and to get to know her away from campus. Not a bad thing.

CHAPTER 4

Third Day of Class

I gave my obligatory lecture about the 14th Amendment and its importance. I explained how originally the Bill of Rights applied only to the federal government until the passage of the 14th Amendment after the Civil War.

When the 14th Amendment was enacted it prohibited the States from denying due process. Due process became defined as a violation of one or more of the rights guaranteed by the Bill of Rights. Thus, after the passage of the 14th Amendment, the Bill of Rights would be applied to the States as well as the federal government.

Students began leaving the class. I thought that Ms. Shaw might have forgotten about our discussion at the end of the last class. No such luck. She approached my desk and said:

"Have you thought about the Tammy Fitzgerald case we talked about after the last class?"

I replied, "I have. It is a fascinating case, but I don't think that I have the expertise you need for such a complicated matter."

"You're the most qualified in this town."

"But we have no access to police files or records, DNA, other forensic evidence, phone or email records, witness statements, blood evidence, clothing, or any of the other things we need to conduct a decent investigation. Really, we have nothing except your suspicions."

"I think that I can get us much of the material that you think we need."

"How would you do that?"

"I have a friend in the police department."

I added with caution, "But he can't share that information with us without getting into big trouble if he gets caught."

She replied, "I'll manage that. Are you in?"

I said, "Well let's meet so you can tell me everything you know. We could meet tomorrow, Wednesday night, around 7:30."

"Ok. I was thinking Smiley's Bar might be good. It's a bar way out on the interstate. No one from school goes there."

"Ok. I'll google the address and see you there tomorrow at 7:30."

Again, I was stepping into the breach. Did she have something to say or was she just another pretty face?

Taylor asked, "Do you want my number?"

"No thank you," I replied.

She seemed a little flustered. "No thank you? Why?"

"Over my years as a criminal prosecutor, I have found that communicating by telephone is a sure-fire way to either get caught or at least arouse suspicion. I cannot tell you how many times I have been able to throw the net over associates because of the electronic trail of a telephone call, text message, or email.

"Even with burner phones, a good investigator is able to find out where the phone was purchased, check video cameras, and connect perpetrators.

"At least for now, I would suggest no electronic communication. Class meets twice a week. We can talk after class which should provide us with a way to set up face-to-face meetings.

She said that she understood. I presumed that she did.

CHAPTER 5

Smiley's Bar

I took off for Smiley's at around a quarter to seven. I headed out onto the interstate. Several miles down the road I saw a free-standing building, set back from the highway. A bright neon sign announced that it was Smiley's. Another slightly smaller neon sign said that cocktails and food were served.

The area around the front and both sides of the building appeared to be for parking. Motorcycles were parked on the west side, and a variety of muscle cars with different paint jobs were parked in the front.

I parked my Chevy Malibu in front. There was a short porch outside of the front exterior wall. I went up two stairs, crossed the porch, and entered through the front door.

As I entered, I looked around and remember remarking to myself, 'What a dive.'

I was a little early. One of the waitresses came over to see if I wanted a table. She was wearing jean shorts, an open western shirt with snaps, and cowboy boots. The other patrons were in cowboy attire with jeans and boots. Boy did I look out of place in a button-down shirt and dress shoes.

"May I help you?" She asked.

"Yes," I replied.

When one enters the room, there is a long bar along the rear wall. On the west side, there are two pool tables. On the east side, there are booths with tall wooden backs. Tables were scattered around the room.

"Would you like a booth?"

"Yes."

She took me to a booth at the far side of the room.

I said, "I'm waiting for another person. A young lady."

She replied, "Your secret's safe with me. I'll bring her over when she arrives."

"Thank you."

The room was very dark. This was not done necessarily for atmosphere but to hide some of the imperfections in the room, of which there were many.

I saw Taylor come in through the front door, which was quite a distance away. She approached the same waitress who sat me. When my eyes finally became adjusted, I saw that she was dressed quite differently than at school. She was wearing a short jean skirt, a tank top, a leather jacket, complete with multiple zippers, and motorcycle-type boots. She could pass for a member of a motorcycle gang.

She was brought over to my table.

"Please sit." I said.

"Thank you."

The booth was semi-circular with a high back and a curved bench seat in dark red faux leather. She sat fairly close to me.

"You look different than at school. Or should I say you are dressed differently."

At school, she dressed similarly to all the other teenage girls in painfully short shorts, a tank top, and flip flops.

She opened, "I have a slightly different life than most of the other students. I am a little older. I was out of school for a year, and during that time, I developed some different friends, other than the few friends I had in high school. Just for full disclosure, I became quite friendly with several motorcycle types. One of my closest friends is a guy named Moose. He is sort of the unofficial leader of the local chapter of a motorcycle association. I became close with him, his wife, and other members of the association.

"I'll tell you all about Moose and his friends later. For now, I would like us to focus in on the Tammy Fitzgerald case.

"When I started babysitting Tammy, she was just 12. Her family had just moved into the largest house in the new subdivision of Haven Lakes. Their house was not only in the subdivision but was in a part of the subdivision reserved for the larger homes. It was by far the largest and most grand home in the entire project.

"The subdivision was not really in Haven but in Newton. Between Haven and Newton, there was a mountain pass with a small, mountain road. Originally, the road was not very good. This isolated Newton. Haven was considered a big city for this area. Newton was considered farmland.

"Around the time that the subdivision, which became known as Haven Lake, was being built, the interstate was taken through the pass near the existing mountain road, greatly improving traffic between Haven and Newton and greatly increasing the value of Newton real estate and all of the real estate past Newton. The subdivision was called Haven Lakes to capitalize on the Haven name, although it was technically located in Newton.

"Newton remained a farming community. Haven was more of a commercial center. The subdivision really serviced Haven."

I interjected, "I remember hearing about this when I was living and working in Haven. My parents moved to Newton just after I started practicing law in Haven. I went to Newton several times to visit. It was really a bear getting through the pass before the interstate was finished. The road was not only narrow but ran along the edge of a steep hillside tapering down into a ravine.

"Otherwise, Newton was a nice place. I really liked the farming aspect. But I didn't know then that one day I would be living and working there after my parents passed."

I continued, "As I recall, the Tammy Fitzgerald kidnapping took place when I just started with the DA's office in Haven. The investigation of the crime was being handled by the Haven-Newton Police Department. They didn't ask for help from the FBI, though it was sorely needed. The DA did not usually get involved until there was a suspect to charge, and in this case, there were no suspects. Besides, I was so new to the department that I would probably not have been asked to participate anyway.

"Looking at it now, Haven Lakes seemed to be a little fancy for the area, particularly the nicer homes within the private part of the subdivision. Was Mr. Fitzgerald doing that kind of business? I heard he was a real estate broker."

Taylor responded, "He was originally a real estate broker working for one of the big realtors in Haven. Sort of a small fish in a small pond. He apparently got some breaks and set up his own shop. Between the new business and the new house, he must have had some good luck. I heard that he was involved in arranging the financing and permits for Haven Lakes."

I remember thinking to myself that though Taylor is very smart and pretty advanced for her age, she really didn't have much feel for how money works or how to accumulate it. I think that she was not entirely in touch with how Mr. Fitzgerald came into such good fortune, which made two of us.

Taylor continued, "Haven Lakes is a typical subdivision. It has a guard gate. It has several man-made lakes also used for the golf course. The basic houses outside of the more expensive homes were cookie-cutter types with stucco exteriors and tile roofs. A few different facades were mixed in. The yards are small.

"The more expensive houses are McMansion types, with vast, custom-appearing facades, fancy doors and windows, pools, spas, and large yards.

"The Fitzgerald house is located in a privately sub-gated area within the subdivision, towards the rear of the property. I guess the lesser houses were used to create a buffer zone. The streets did not run at right angles but circled around with several cul-de-sacs.

"Somehow, Mr. Fitzgerald managed to get the largest and by far the most expensive home in the entire tract.

"He and his family moved in before the house was really complete, even before the guard shack was up and running. I was invited over to babysit for Tammy when her parents went into Haven for dinner and, sometimes, a movie. I was recommended by one of the secretaries in his real estate office. The subdivision was brand new, and many of the homes were not occupied.

"Right after they moved in, while Tammy was still 12, she disappeared. I was not babysitting that day, thank God."

I interjected, "Were there any suspects?"

"I'm getting to that. Tammy had a mother, Diane, a father, Don, and an older brother, Jason. Initially, they were all suspects. I believe that this is not unusual."

I broke in and, as usual, pontificated, "Typically the family members will be considered the first suspects. They would, of course, have contact with the victim, as they would all be living together. They would be known to have disagreements, as is not unusual among families. Tammy would be reaching the age where she and her mother would be beginning to disagree about her attire, her constant use of her cell phone, her way of dressing, her homework, her contact with boys, and all the other typical incidents of the mother-daughter drama

"I have often wondered why the police would think that these types of family arguments would lead to murder. Siblings would often be suspected due to sibling rivalry. Another non-starter for me anyway.

"Fathers get the worst of it. Somehow some twisted sexual tension would be considered a motive. I would like to think that those feelings would be extremely rare, except to someone on the outside looking in."

I then asked Taylor if she had heard about whether any specific family members were considered suspects, or if there were any non-related suspects. I asked if there was any physical evidence, or if there were any other theories being floated.

She said that she did not know much. It was thought that the father or brother might have taken her from her room, taken her away, and hidden the body. The police figured that she was murdered, as no remains were found.

Though new, the subdivision had a patrol service. No one saw anything on the night of the disappearance. The houses, though large, were fairly close together with good views to the adjacent properties, but many were still not occupied.

I asked Taylor if anyone considered an outsider. There must be another way of getting in and out of the subdivision, other than the front gate. One would presume that the fire department would require at least one or perhaps two additional locations where one might leave or enter the project.

Also, houses this large would require a regular gardener who would probably know more about ingress and egress than even the owners. This type of staff might know someone, who knows someone, who might use this information to gain access.

I asked, "Was anyone other than the family questioned?"

Taylor responded, "I did not hear of any other people being questioned, but I was not following the law enforcement developments closely at that time, and the police did not appear anxious to share."

I replied, "Well it is going to be necessary to not only identify but also to question other suspects. If this is not possible, we are just spinning our wheels."

I asked, "Was DNA evidence collected?"

"As I recall," Taylor mused, "It was said that the DNA gathered was not in a sufficient quantity to be useful."

"How about phone records?"

"I don't know, but I think I could find out. I know someone at the police department."

I continued, "Are there cameras around the subdivision?"

Taylor replied that she did not know but that she thought that it was possible.

I went on, "Well, let's look at this realistically. The crime scene by now has been completely cleaned and cannot provide any evidence. Fingerprints are long gone. There may be some tiny amount of material for DNA, but advanced techniques will be needed to make sense of it, if that is even possible. If someone other than a family member did this, he or she could be long gone from Haven by this time and might not even be in CODIS.

"This leaves us with phone records, possible video evidence, whatever was put into the evidence locker, and advanced DNA testing.

"So, if you can get phone records for the family and everyone associated with the family, video evidence from cameras around the subdivision, and access to the evidence in the evidence locker, we might have a place from which to start. Without at least these items, we should probably forget about it.

"I will work on the new DNA techniques."

"This all seems to be a tall order," Taylor replied. I do know someone in the police department. A young guy who started around the time of the kidnapping, but who was too green to be involved in such an important case. His name is Frank Diaz."

"Okay, I'll see you in our next class. Don't be late."

We both left the bar, got into our respective cars, and drove off. I went home. I can't speak for Taylor.

I was smitten. I was so hoping that she would be a bore with little or nothing to say and that all of the kidnapping suspicion was just so much high school drama. If this had been so, I could politely say that the case was too cold to pursue and that it would be impossible to assemble any credible evidence at this late date.

This was not to be. Even though I thought the chances of success were slim, there was just enough there to keep digging, particularly since my new partner was so intriguing. In short, working with her would be enough to keep me interested.

CHAPTER 6
Officer Frank Diaz

At this time, Officer Frank Diaz had been with the Haven-Newton Police Department for a few months.

He came on board just after the Tammy Fitzgerald kidnapping. This was good for the seasoned detectives and administrators already working on the case as it would make it easier to exclude him from participating.

Frank was a local boy. He was born in Newton and worked on his parents' farm picking and hauling oranges. Frank and his family had that old-fashioned work ethic.

Frank and Taylor met when they were both bringing oranges to the central produce market in Newton to be picked up by a food broker and taken to Haven for additional distribution.

He was 18. She was only 16. They began talking, which was rare for her, as at this point in her life, she was suspicious of men generally. She had no relationship with her father. And she always felt that men would consider her to be easy in light of her being a farm girl from poor circumstances. She was understandably a little frightened of men. I have to confess that some of this still lingers with her and was fortified by her relationship with her mother, ever the competitor with her daughter.

But Frank would have nothing to do with all of that. He was the first man-person who she felt did not judge her based on her appearance and circumstances.

Even though by 16 she was becoming beautiful, Frank seemed to be able to bypass all of that and relate to her on another level, one orange farm person to another. Good parental training? Strong religious beliefs? A little of both? Hard to say.

They began meeting. The meetings became longer. They could talk for hours even though neither of them could be away from his or her respective farm for too long.

Frank told her of his dream to enter the police academy and become a full-time police person with the Haven-Newton Police Department.

She was only 16, so her future plans were not that immediate. She still had time to figure out what she wanted to do with her life. She told Frank that she knew that she wanted to go to college. She was interested in nursing, accounting, law, business. Many things.

He was her greatest cheerleader. He encouraged her to follow her heart and continued to remind her that she could be whatever she wanted to be, a welcome switch from being constantly put down by her mother. He was probably the first person to instill in her a legitimate feeling of self-confidence.

Little did she know that the lessons that she learned from Frank would, in the future, be applied to her relationships with others. They would make her a better person. The kind of person that she became.

Their relationship became solid but not romantic. Frank was a good-looking boy, but he was 18, and she was only 16. They could not go there either by law or otherwise. She was too young to take a step towards the romantic, except perhaps with another 16-year-old, and she did not know anyone that age who was at all interesting. This might be a circumstance where their respective ages were working against them. It would be hard to believe that Frank was not interested.

Fortunately for both of them, before they could do anything that they would regret, Frank left Newton to attend the police academy. The academy was located in Haven. He would text Taylor now and then to see how she was doing. He never returned to Newton to live. He became engrossed in learning police procedure and then working in the department as a rookie.

I think that deep down he felt that if he returned to Newton after Taylor reached 18, he might make a fool of himself. A Latin guy with a white girl in this part of the world. Little did he know that his race or religion had absolutely no meaning to her. But this was lost on him because it seemed so important to everyone else. He was kind, nurturing, gentle, and all of the things that make a regular guy a complete failure with women.

I will say this, however, that when Taylor called him for help with the kidnapping case, he was quick to meet and offer any assistance that he could. It was pretty obvious that he still carried a torch for her, but it was also obvious that her interest, at least presently, was in the case. Again, poor timing for him.

If it means anything to anyone, I like him. Not just because he pulled himself up from his own boot straps to leave the fields and become a policeman, but because of his legitimate feelings for her. I probably should have been jealous, but I just could not bring myself to go there. If she chose him in the end, that would be a relationship worth supporting.

CHAPTER 7

Moose

Though Taylor was 19, to a grown man such as Moose, she seemed pretty intelligent for her years. While the other girls were concerned with their makeup, clothes, shoes and all of the newest night clubs and hot spots, Taylor had different priorities. More real. More serious. Not frivolous. Learning her history, I could see why.

Taylor's father left her and her mother when Taylor was 10. By the time she was 12, out of necessity, her mother had her working. Her mother, who did not know much about anything, was able to teach her just enough to allow her to learn from outside sources.

Through trial and error, some advice she solicited from the family accountant, and reading as many books on business operations on which she could get her hands, she eventually learned how to run the farm, notwithstanding her mother constantly putting her down.

She learned how to organize the planting, harvesting, and shipping. She learned how to contract labor, pay everyone, make out all of the tax forms and agricultural reports, and do all of the things necessary.

This was essential so she could make enough money to keep the farm going while her mother pursued her full-time avocation of drinking. By the time Taylor was 14, her mother had become a full- blown alcoholic and totally dependent on Taylor.

Having to support herself and keep the farm going meant no time to party or to compare outfits with the other girls, girls who were taken care of by their families, as would be normal at this stage of their lives. Taylor, on the other hand, was all business. I have to confess that I found it intriguing, though a typical 19-year-old boy or girl might find it boring.

How is it that a beautiful girl can draw you into her problems just by telling you about them? Once you hear that a beautiful girl has a problem, you immediately want to help. If taking on her problems is the only way you have to get close to her, you take them on. It's an age-old-phenomena.

I was more than willing to take on Taylor's problems. I guess I was smitten.

Taylor did not have any conventional school-aged friends. Jocks, cheerleaders, school spirit types were not her style. Her priority was survival. Their priority was having fun.

Taylor seemed to enjoy the local motorcycle types more than her school mates. I came to find out that her closest friend was a gentleman by the name of Giovanni Moustaka, also known as Moose.

Taylor was introduced to Moose by a friend of her mother's. Moose was under an IRS audit, and it did not look good. Her mother's friend told Moose that Taylor was pretty good with bookkeeping and that she might be able to help.

The IRS auditor told Moose that he had so greatly understated his income that it appeared as if fraud charges were going to be brought. In reality, Moose's idiot accountant, rather than computing his income from bank records, estimated his income, and his estimate was way too low.

Taylor, being a clever girl, calculated his actual income. She then figured out his actual legal deductions. After subtracting his actual legal deductions from his actual income, his taxable income was not too much more than the accountant's guess.

Moose paid less than $1,000.00 in taxes, penalties, and interest, and the fraud charges were dropped. He was tickled and appreciative.

After that, Taylor handled all of Moose's business affairs.

Moose was the president of the local chapter of the Motorcycle Enthusiasts of America, or MEA. MEA solicited members who paid modest annual dues. For their dues, they would receive a decal for their bikes, a membership card, and access to two meetings a year. The members looked out for one another.

Each member was tasked with letting the other members know about speed traps, overzealous enforcement of muffler violations, road conditions, etc.

Moose also ran a mail order business where he offered T shirts, jackets, coffee mugs, and cup holders sporting the MEA logo.

Taylor was instrumental in helping Moose with the business. She did all of the book work, took photos of the merchandise, placed ads on the internet, filled the ads, collected the money, paid suppliers, and gave the profits to Moose.

Moose was really fond of Taylor. She was like a daughter to him, and she considered him to be a father figure. Moose introduced Taylor to other members of his organization who also liked her, and whom she also helped. There was really nothing not to like. She was pleasant, not full of herself, helpful in any way she could be, and, just for extra measure, pretty too.

CHAPTER 8

Fourth Day of Class

Class met as usual. Unfortunately, I did not feel well and had to cancel class after trying to start my lecture.

The students filed out. As is typical, the students were fine with the cancelation. They would have an additional hour and a half to pursue their social agendas.

"Okay class, sorry to cancel on you. We will meet again next week. Hopefully after a couple of days and the weekend, I will feel better."

Taylor lingered, as had become her custom. She inquired about my health. I said it was just a cold and a sore throat. She said that she had some other business with Moose's wife, Carol, to take care of, and that she could use some time away from the case.

I was fine with it.

CHAPTER 9

Carol

Moose and Carol were married 15 years ago. He was 30 and she was 25 when they met. Initially, Moose sort of took her in. Eventually, their friendship grew into love, and, ultimately, after five years, they got married. Carol is now 45. Moose served in Desert Storm which would make him around 50.

Until she met Taylor, Carol really lacked the acumen to help Moose out with the business. This was difficult for her and was hard on their relationship. All of the pressure was on Moose, all of the time. It seemed alright at the beginning, but a good marriage is built on a partnership where both parties are able to pitch in, even if each person can't do everything as well as the other.

One would think that Taylor had the looks and countenance of a girl whom Carol would immediately hate. She was beautiful, smart, great with the business, great with people, and liked by Moose and his friends. All of the things to which Carol aspired.

But if you thought that Taylor was the type of person to set up a competition between her and Carol, your ignorance would be showing. She was way too smart for that.

Taylor went to great lengths to make Carol feel valuable, to never flirt with Moose or any of the others for that matter, and to downplay her looks in favor of being a helpmate for anyone who needed help.

Her instinct was to work with Carol to try to show her how to take care of the books and the internet business, starting with very small steps. She was able to do this in such a way that she did not seem phony or to be trying too hard.

Eventually, as time passed, Carol began to get the hang of the business and, with some gentle encouragement, she even began researching products to sell in the on-line store, with the end result of actually selling some.

This greatly improved Carol's feeling of self-worth and made her relationship with Moose more of an equal partnership than a caretaking venture. Also, with Carol being able to help took some of the pressure off of Moose.

Taylor accomplished her mission with Carol barely knowing her objective, which was only to help Carol, to help Moose, and to help as many others as she could. A pretty neat trick.

The relationship between Taylor and Carol grew into a legitimate friendship. They hung out and talked about things woman-to-woman. This was good for both of them, particularly since Taylor did not have a mother with whom to share.

During one of their long chats Carol asked Taylor, "I heard that you might have met a guy, or maybe even two, you are interested in."

For Taylor, this was completely out of the blue. In fact, it was so far outside of the realm of possibility that she was flabbergasted.

Taylor replied, "Where on earth did you hear that?"

"You know that we all hang out at Smiley's, and me and Moose know everybody in there. I heard this from one of the waitresses. I think she was a little jealous. She said that both of the guys are good looking and that they only pay attention to you. I guess that means that they don't pay attention to her. She implied that she tried many times, unsuccessfully, to get the attention of either one of them but was unsuccessful. You know you have the reputation of never being interested in anyone. While good and all, sometimes it makes women a little suspicious and men a little frustrated."

"I'm sorry. That is not my intention. Actually, my life is such a mess right now that I'm not even thinking about guys."

"Okay. I guess I can live with that."

"If you must know, I do occasionally meet with two guys there because they are helping me with a case. I don't know if you remember but several months ago a young girl by the name of Tammy Fitzgerald was kidnapped. I was her babysitter. No ransom demand was ever made, and her body was never found. I thought that the police investigation was handled so poorly that I took it upon myself to learn more. The white guy is one of my teachers. He is an attorney and worked in the DA's office in Haven.

"The other guy, a couple of years younger, is a police officer in the same precinct that investigated the kidnapping in the first place."

Allowing the story of the kidnapping to go in one ear and out the other, Carol replied, "So, nothing is going on? I mean with the two guys."

Taylor replied, "Yes, nothing is going on."

Carol left it with, "If anything changes, you let me know. I'd like to see you find someone you like."

"I'll let you know."

Just then Moose came in.

"What are you two up to? Looks like an intense conversation."

"I was just telling Carol about a kidnapping case I have been looking into."

Moose replied, "What happened? Can I help?"

Taylor continued, "It was several months ago. It was the case of the little girl who was kidnapped from her parents' home in Haven Lakes. I was her babysitter, but not on the night she was kidnapped. No ransom demand was made. No body was found. The police did such a poor job I thought I would look into it. I've enlisted one of my teachers and an off-duty cop I know."

Moose replied, "Keep me posted on it." Moose was not the kind of guy who would force his way into someone else's situation, but he made you know that he would be there if you needed him.

Out of left field, Moose asked, "I know it's short notice, but this weekend me and some of the boys are going camping. I'd love it if you would come along. You can learn about guns and hand-to-hand combat. Everyone going was in the military and really knows the ropes. You'll be learning from the best. Most of them were special forces, Seals, Rangers, like that."

Taylor's reply shocked Carol and even surprised Moose a little when she said, "That actually sounds like fun. I could use a couple of days away from this madness. Where and when?"

"Rock Ridge National Park. We will be leaving from Smiley's at 5 a.m. on Friday and will return Sunday evening."

Taylor's replied, "I'll see you Friday at 5."

CHAPTER 10
Camping

Taylor awoke at 4 a.m., pulled on a pair of jeans, put on a long sleeve shirt, got into her hiking boots, and tucked her hair into a baseball cap.

She arrived at Smiley's just before 5. Moose and a few of his friends were already there.

They were quite a group. Most of the guys were around 50. They were veterans of Desert Storm. There were a couple of Vietnam vets. They were in their early 70's.

They all rode chopped motorcycles with chromed engine parts. All of the bikes were outfitted with holders for camping gear and guns. Most of the bikes were black. There were 15 in all.

There were two other ladies in the group. Taylor came over to the group, and Moose introduced her to everyone.

Rather than going back through Haven and Newton, Moose decided to drive to the north entrance of the park. The north entrance was closer to the rocky hiking area and the particular camp site that Moose and his friends liked.

Taylor rode on Moose's bike. Carol stayed home to tend to the business, as she learned enough from Taylor to sort of handle things herself, at least for a few days.

The bikes roared in unison as they traveled in perfect formation. The roads to the north entrance of the park were pretty good.

Upon arriving at the park entrance, Moose and the group checked in with the park ranger telling him that they intended to hike and camp along the north ridge. This meant that they would have to park in a parking area on flat ground and hike up to their destination.

Up on the ridge, there was a developed camping area with a bathroom and running water. They would make camp when they arrived and leave from there for some sight-seeing, hunting, fishing, and other activities.

They parked. They hiked up to the north ridge camping area. This part of the terrain was for tourists. It was a pretty easy hike. Some of the areas beyond the campgrounds would be much more difficult to negotiate.

When they arrived at the campgrounds, they moved to the area assigned to them by the ranger. It looked pretty good and was not too far from an outhouse.

It was now around midday. The group set up tents, tables, and umbrellas. It was lunch time, and everybody worked together to prepare the food, serve the food, and clear the tables. Everybody worked. Taylor neither asked for nor received any favorable treatment for being a girl or for being a first-timer. This is how she preferred it anyway.

After lunch, Moose asked Taylor, "Would you like to learn how to shoot?"

Taylor replied, "Remember Moose, I am a farm girl. I've been shooting since I was eleven years' old. I have a 22."

Moose replied, "No offense, but isn't that sort of a toy gun. My interest is whether you want to learn to shoot a real gun."

Taylor responded, "Very funny. But yes, I would like to learn about other guns."

"Okay. Let me introduce you to Lester. He's a gun specialist. We served together in Desert Storm. He repairs guns. The guys that fix them tend to know more than the guys who only shoot them. Hey Lester, can you come over here a minute?"

Lester came over to Moose and Taylor. Moose inquired, "Lester, do you have time to take Taylor here shooting?"

"Sure."

He was apparently a man of few words.

Taylor and Lester hit one of the hiking trails. Lester was armed with an AR 15 and a Beretta pistol. That made him pretty much ready for anything.

About 30 minutes up the mountain from camp, they came into a clearing with good visibility in all directions. The weather was clear. A good place and time for shooting.

Taylor asked, "What do I do? I have shot before, but only a 22."

Lester replied, "Less is probably better. Let's hope that you haven't developed too many bad habits. In shooting, you must always remain focused on what you are doing. You cannot let your mind wander or you might hurt yourself or someone else.

"You will need to use the proper grip and keep your body in the proper position. Don't anticipate or flinch from the recoil. The recoil is going to happen, so no heeling.

"When holding a gun, never point it at yourself when holstering, never hold the gun up for too long or your arms will get tired, and never hold a gun next to your ear, like you see in the movies. If you hold a pistol, for example, next to your ear and fire it, you might lose some of your hearing."

Taylor could not believe how thorough and knowledgeable Lester was. Also, she appreciated that he was all business. She was there to learn about guns, and that was all.

Lester had Taylor start with the Beretta. She kept the gun in front of her, did not hold it up for too long, squeezed the trigger, and shot. The recoil happened, but she handled it without too much flinching.

Lester said, "That was pretty good. I like the fact that your grip and body position are good. If you do those things wrong, they are hard to re-learn."

Lester showed her the AR 15, a killing machine. For a gun that inflicts this kind of damage, it is known for causing less recoil, which, for Taylor's purposes, is a good thing. Lester explained that more recoil makes the shooting less accurate, as the gun tends to pull up when fired. Lester explained that some of the rifles that the military uses, like the M4, are not legal to use.

She shot the AR 15 at a far-away target and had some decent results. Both she and Lester were pretty happy with the shooting lesson. They returned to camp. Evening was coming, and they would be making dinner soon.

As with lunch, everyone worked together to make dinner, serve the food, and clean up the mess. No passes. Taylor was thinking to herself that one of the great things about the military is that it makes everybody work together towards a common goal, even if it is a minor goal. She was thinking how much this would benefit some of the young and immature guys she knew from school.

As everyone had been up early that morning, when 9:30 came around, they were ready to turn in. By 10, everyone was in his or her sleeping bag, asleep.

The group woke up at around 7 on Saturday. It was another desert morning with long orange shadows cast on the rocks.

They all got up, made breakfast, and cleaned up.

Moose asked Taylor if she would like to learn about hand-to-hand combat. She said that she would. Moose motioned for a gentleman to come over and said, "Bart, this is Taylor. She says that she would like to learn about hand-to-hand combat. Could you help her with that?"

"I will certainly try."

Bart was a little older than most of the crew. It turned out that he was a Vietnam vet who had seen much action in that very deadly conflict.

Bart was a man of few words, not unlike nearly all of the men on this trip. These men were the type who allowed their actions to do their talking; they did not need to add anything by using words. Taylor sized Bart up. To her, he seemed like a nice guy willing to be helpful.

Interestingly enough, much later, Taylor learned from Moose that Bart was the most decorated Green Beret in his outfit. As for his resume in hand-to-hand combat, he had so many kills that they finally had to make him an instructor. Sort of speaks for itself.

Taylor and Bart set out for the steeper hills. It was a very tough hike, even for a 19-year-old farm girl. It was barely a workout for Bart, however. One would have thought that he was taking a stroll down the Champs-Elysees.

They arrived at a nice clearing by the stream coming down the mountain. Taylor indicated that this seemed as good a place as any to get started.

Bart kicked things off with a little background. Bart told Taylor that each branch of the services engaged in hand-to-hand combat, on at least some level, but that each branch seemed to gravitate towards a particular type.

Bart listed the various types including: Boxing, Muay Thai, Brazilian Jiu Jitsu, Karate, Taekwondo, Systema, and Krav Maga.

Green Berets were trained primarily to kill. Killing was also an immediate objective for the Marines. The Seals liked Krav Maga, a form of martial arts used by the Israeli Mossad.

Bart thought it was time for a demonstration. He would use a feigned combat situation to show Taylor some moves. All 110 pounds of Taylor squared off against Bart, who was six feet, two inches, and 220 pounds of solid muscle. Let's give Bart the size advantage.

Bart showed Taylor how to stand. Bart explained to Taylor that if you expect that it is possible that a physical altercation might break out, it is important to keep your hands up, because the time it takes to raise your hands could be less than the time it takes to get knocked out.

He said that the hands should be open with the left hand slightly higher than the right. The reason for this, he said, was the likelihood that your opponent will open with a right cross. The left hand would be used to deflect it away from your face while opening up the opponent's face for contact by your right hand.

You might try to slide your right arm along your opponent's neck, with a backhand motion, moving him away. You might grab his arm and twist it, causing him to fall to the ground.

Once your opponent is on the ground, several stomping techniques may be used, either to the body or the throat.

The throat is vulnerable. When standing, pressure may be exerted on the neck which can be fatal. A palm strike at the face can be disabling. Eye gouging and fish-hooking may be used to grab the eyes, nose, and mouth and pull until the opponent is disabled.

Bart then, unbelievably, moved to the philosophical. He told Taylor that because of physiology and environment, women fight differently than men.

When little boys grow up, at a very early age they learn how to throw a ball. A boy throws a ball over his shoulder, turning his hips and legs, extending his back, and pronating his wrist. This technique is first applied in baseball and then in football. It is then transferred to boxing. When someone throws a right hand in boxing, he turns his hip in the direction of the thrust of his arm.

This method of turning the hip along with the throwing of the arm allows a person to apply the core of his body to the delivery, and the core is much stronger than the arm alone.

Girls, on the other hand, do not always get this instruction and might deliver with more of the arm than the body. Also, from the standpoint of physiology, the upper body of a girl is probably going to weaker than that of a man. Bart reminded Taylor that these were just generalizations.

According to Bart, the upper body disparity lends itself to women learning to do more with their legs than their arms. Where men might get their power from the core, women develop their power from their extremely strong upper legs. They can kick high and hard, and they do so in most of the martial arts.

Bart felt that for a woman to get low and sweep the legs was an effective tool and might serve her better than facing off in a boxing match against a man. Bart told her that he had seen women in Vietnam sweep the leg, and when the man went down, stomp the groin. A very effective (and painful I might add) technique.

Taylor and Bart spent the rest of the afternoon with Bart showing Taylor how to sweep the leg, stomp the groin, finger the eyes, strike the throat, and generally destroy an average person.

Bart explained that interestingly enough grabbing and holding someone's wrists can be effective and that when someone comes up and grabs you from behind, you can pull under their arms, twist, and then pull them to the ground.

In closing, Bart reminded her that among professional fighters, it was he who could take the most punishment who tended to be the most revered and was often the most successful.

She knew that she would never be an MMA fighter, but she felt better about fending for herself. Just the ability to learn how to deflect and sweep was well worth the time.

Taylor and Bart headed back to camp. It was Saturday night, and the program was to make a large dinner and to share stories by the camp fire. Taylor had heard that some of the stories about time spent in-country in far-away places could get pretty gruesome.

Dinner, as usual, was a form of barbequed meat. Taylor was not a big meat person, but this was what was available. She ate everything with no complaints. By the way, there were no complainers in the group. No surprise. Remember, all of these guys spent at least two years in the blazing heat or the freezing cold of a jungle or a desert.

After dinner, the campfire was lit. A couple of guys Taylor did not know shared their stories of their time in the service.

One was a swift boat captain during Vietnam. He enlightened the audience with stories of motoring up the river with only a few guns hoping to at least get a look at a Viet Cong soldier. Their job was to draw out the enemy. The Viet Cong were embedded so deeply that you would swear that there was no one even there.

Truly a war that was lost because more of enemy was willing to die than we were willing to kill.

The next person told of his time in Kuwait removing the Iraqis, never knowing if Saddam Hussein would gas them. Just the thought could really keep you up at night.

Moose asked Taylor if she would like to share a story. She said that after hearing the harrowing stories of some of her fellow campers, her story would seem trivial. Moose urged her.

Taylor told the story of Tammy Fitzgerald's kidnapping. She relayed that she had been the child's babysitter.

She said that the child was taken from her room at three or four in the morning when the parents were in the house. She was not discovered missing until the next day when she did not join them for breakfast. The little girl was only 12.

Time went by, and no ransom demand was made, and no body was found. They ultimately had a funeral, and the child's mother nearly had a breakdown. It was really bad.

She told them that the father had come into some money as he was alleged to have been instrumental in getting the financing and building permits for the new subdivision at Haven Lakes. He was also given the largest and most expensive home in the development and the right to sell the rest of the homes.

She told everyone that the police did what she considered to be a poor job of investigating the case. There was no video. There was no DNA evidence. The search was minimal. And the detective in charge retired.

She told everyone that she had enlisted the help of her professor, an attorney, and a junior police officer, a friend.

She said that she intended to visit the recorder's office in Bryan, visit the retired detective, find a new DNA lab, and do whatever was necessary to either find Tammy or get justice for her. She told her enraptured audience 'If I have to do it all myself, I will.'

The group applauded. Two or three of the men asked if they could help. She cleverly let them know that she needed more evidence before she needed help but that when the evidence was available, she would contact them. She took their phone numbers.

Everyone turned in about 10. Everyone was up the next morning at 7. Breakfast was made and cleaned up. This would be a half-day. They would leave in the afternoon so they could get home by dinner time on Sunday.

After breakfast, Moose found Taylor. He asked her if she would like to learn about torture and waterboarding. It just so happened that they had someone knowledgeable in the field along for the trip.

She was interested and said yes.

Taylor was then introduced to a very scary figure. His real name was not known. He was only known as the "Doctor of Pain." After giving his little speech and demonstration, even the guys attending this seminar, guys who had seen torture and death beyond what a human could possibly imagine, were shocked. For the Doctor, of course, it was just business as usual.

The Doctor went over some of the classics: The Rack, the Brazen Bull, the Iron Maiden, and the Pear of Anguish. He also included the generic: Dunking, boiling, freezing, burning, burying alive, restraining, and feeding to the animals.

He described how some of them operated. The Rack is used to pull the limbs of the victim apart from his body. The Brazen Bull consists of a chamber in which one is locked before being burned to death.

The particularly gruesome Iron Maiden was next up. It is a chamber about the size of a coffin. Inside it has multiple sharp probes. A person is placed in the chamber, and the chamber's walls are slowly drawn in to a point where the probes begin to pierce the skin. If the needed information is not given, the probes are allowed to go deeper.

The Pear of Anguish is a metal device consisting of leaves controlled by a bolt. As the bolt is turned, the leaves separate from one another. The device is placed into an orifice, and the bolt is turned. As the leaves separate, the inside of the orifice is pulled apart, causing death.

Dunking, boiling, freezing, burning, burying alive, etc., though self-explanatory, were explained by the Doctor in great detail, much to his delight.

The Doctor then moved on to waterboarding. He said that he barely considers waterboarding to be torture. As for its history, in 2008, Congress enacted a bill banning waterboarding. President George W. Bush vetoed the bill. Congress lacked the votes to override the veto, so waterboarding stayed.

In 2009, President Barack Obama signed an Executive Order effectively banning the use of waterboarding.

As the Doctor explained, with waterboarding a person is strapped to a board which is tilted backwards. A cloth is placed over the person's face. Water is run onto the cloth and into the nose, the sinus cavity, and the mouth of the detainee.

This gives the detainee the sensation of drowning, and will cause drowning if it is carried on for too long.

The Doctor explained to us that as a way of beating waterboarding, some people have advocated holding one's breath. Unfortunately, however, the nose is still open, and water will reach the sinus cavity whether one's breath is held or not.

The Doctor went on to say that if one is really serious about beating waterboarding, he would first have to achieve the ability to survive with a sinus cavity full of water. If one can get to that point, he might be able to beat it.

The Doctor suggested that if one could survive with a sinus cavity full of water, he or she might then pretend to be drowning to encourage his interrogators to stop, so as not to kill him before obtaining the information they need.

The Doctor suggested that someone try waterboarding to see if it was really that bad. It seems as if he never goes anywhere, even camping, without his waterboarding kit.

Taylor volunteered. The guys objected. But she was determined to try.

The Doctor was kind enough to strap Taylor to his waterboarding plank. With the help of a couple of the guys, the plank, and Taylor's head, were tilted backwards.

The Doctor placed a cloth over her face and poured water through the cloth and into her mouth and nose. After a few seconds, she panicked, trying to spew water out of her mouth. The guys tilted her upright so she could expel the water.

She insisted on trying again. She was tilted backwards, her face was covered, and water was poured onto the cloth. This time she allowed her sinuses to fill. Though unpleasant, she allowed herself to become acclimated to having full sinus cavities. After 20 seconds, it was considered as if she had beaten it, and she tapped out. She was a trooper.

The time had now arrived to have lunch and break camp. Everyone returned to the campsite. Lunch was prepared, served, and cleaned up. Everyone packed up his or her sleeping bag, tent, clothing, and other utensils.

The entire campsite was cleaned of each and every piece of paper and scrap of food, leaving the site in better condition than it was in before they arrived. It was their way. Good citizens get invited back.

They made the easy hike back to the parking lot, loaded up their bikes, and headed back to Smiley's.

As Taylor rode back with Moose, she recognized that it was a fun and educational time, but she was more impressed with the guys and gals and how supportive they had been with a newcomer. She hoped that she could, at some point, return the favor.

On Monday, Taylor dropped by my office. With me being sick and out of commission over the weekend, trying not to pry, I asked her how her weekend went.

This, of course, opened the door. She related the whole story, which I found better than if she felt she needed to hide her activities from me. The camping, the food, the shooting, the hand-to-hand combat, and the waterboarding. She went on and on about how great everyone was and how she did her best to stay out of the way.

With friends like this, I pity the fool who crosses Taylor Shaw.

CHAPTER 11

Fifth Day of Class

After four days in bed, I was ready to get out of the house, even if it was only to teach. I started with my promise to connect the Constitution to its history.

I went through the Magna Carta, England's unwritten constitution, the need to increase taxes after the French and Indian War, no taxation without representation, the Boston Massacre, the Boston Tea Party, Lexington and Concord, the Second Continental Congress, George Washington becoming Commander in Chief, the Declaration of Independence, France entering the war, the Articles of Confederation, and the winning of independence in 1783.

Class ended. Students began to file out of the room. Taylor remained.

Taylor started, "I looked into some of the things we spoke about at our last meeting. I am pretty certain that I will be able to get phone records and some articles from the evidence locker for DNA testing."

I replied, "We need to talk more about why you think this is all necessary. Aren't they fairly certain that the child is dead?"

"They are, but I am not. I just have a feeling that there is more to this than meets the eye. Can we meet again?"

"Okay," I replied. She seemed bound and determined to continue her search for the elusive Tammy Fitzgerald, even in the face of all logic, reason, and evidence. She was ferocious and loyal almost to a fault to the people about whom she cared.

Taylor added, "I think I feel the way George Washington must have felt in 1775, but he persevered, got help from anyone who would help him, even the French, and ultimately prevailed. I guess I'm hoping to have his luck. Can we meet again at Smiley's on Wednesday? I don't think you teach that day."

"Yes. Smiley's Wednesday it is."

After she left, I was thinking to myself how much her attitude reminded me of a famous quote from Winston Churchill. When facing overwhelming odds, he said:

"It is not enough that we do our best;
sometimes we must do what is required."

CHAPTER 12

Smiley's Bar

I was a little early. I was seated at a booth in the back as before. Taylor came in and was directed to my table. She joined me.

She started, "I spoke with my contact at the police department, Officer Frank Diaz. I've known him since I was 16. He is really young. He said he could probably get the phone records but that every phone number from everyone in the family, everyone connected to the family, and everyone who could possibly be connected to the crime was checked, and nothing of interest was found.

"According to Frank, the crime was probably committed around three to four o'clock in the morning. As to the family, there were no calls after 8 p.m., either incoming or outgoing. This makes sense since the father has a day job, the mother is a homemaker, and the kids are in school.

"According to Frank, the lead person on the case was Detective Oliver Pratt, a 25-year veteran of the Department, who was up for retirement around the time the crime was being investigated.

"Frank says that he was barely allowed to do anything with the case or even listen to the senior officers talk about the case, as he was brand new to the department.

"Frank did say that he heard that Mr. Fitzgerald's gardener called early in the morning on the day of the kidnapping. It was presumed that he was looking for general instructions as to what needed to be planted or watered. The police considered it likely that he did not even know a crime was committed, as news of the crime was withheld from the media, at least until mid-day.

"One thing that I found interesting was that according to Frank, no ransom demand was ever made. One would think that as kidnapping was such a complicated and dangerous crime, the perpetrator would want first and foremost to get paid for his trouble."

Taylor went on, "Have you ever heard of a kidnapping with no ransom demand? It just seems so unlikely to me."

I replied, "True. But unfortunately, I have. There was a case in Los Angeles 50 years ago where a young woman, Marina Habe, was kidnapped from her mother's driveway. The mother and the police waited for a ransom demand, but it never came. A couple of days later, the young woman was found brutally stabbed to death and thrown down a hill along Mulholland Drive.

"The perpetrators were never found, and, as I mentioned, no ransom demand was ever made. It appears as if the perpetrators just kept the young woman alive for a couple of days for their own purposes, even feeding her, and then threw her away, probably fearing that she could identify them."

"Many magazine articles and blogs have been written about this event, including the book, *The Tragic Death of Marina Habe*, in which the entire case is set out in detail."

"It seems as if whenever the death of Marina is reported, including in this book, the case of a second young woman by the name of Reet Jurvetson is also considered. Reet was about the same age as Marina; she was 19, and Marina was 17. They were both about the same height, 5'6". They both had similar builds.

"Reet too was kidnapped, held, and ultimately thrown down the hill along Mulholland Drive, very close to the location where Marina's body was found.

"In light of these two cases, it cannot be ruled out that Tammy was kidnapped just for the kidnapper's entertainment, as sick as that sounds. It can happen, and it appears as if it has. Whenever the cases of Marina and Reet come up, it seems as if efforts are made to tie them to Charles Manson. Charles Manson was really not in full swing at the time of Marina's death and was in jail at the time of Reet's. But we learn to never say never."

Taylor mentioned that she thought that Frank could secure the evidence from the evidence locker and look into whether video evidence was available.

I asked, "Do you think that Frank would meet with us? I have several questions for him. I don't think that we can get very far without him."

"Sure," Taylor replied.

"See me after class tomorrow and let me know where and when."

"Okay."

CHAPTER 13

Sixth Day of Class

We discussed in detail whether the United States was meant to become a secular or a religious republic.

I submitted that on the secular side, Article IV states that no religious test shall be required as a qualification for office. Also, the First Amendment provides that Congress shall make no law respecting the establishment of a religion.

I pointed out that on the religious side, if one reads the Constitution and the Declaration of Independence together as our founding documents, the reference in the Declaration to a creator could lead one to believe that religion was expected to play a part in the new republic.

I pointed out that it might be interesting to note that the First Amendment only prohibited the new Congress from establishing a national religion for the combined States as the founders feared a national religion similar to the Church of England. However, it did not prohibit a State from establishing one or more State-wide religions within a State, which was contemplated.

I went on that as far as we know, no Supreme Court case has ever cited the Bible as a source of law. Generally, when the question gets too close to religion, the Court will say that the matter is better left to the States; this has been one of the Supreme Court's go-to ways of ducking many difficult decisions on several fronts, not just religious.

Taylor again waited for me after class. I was beginning to think that the other students were becoming suspicious of whatever relationship we might have, or were perceived to have.

She said, "Interesting stuff this business of religion and government. As far as I can tell, even if unintended, religion has crept into the culture and into the interpretation of our law."

I replied, "Religious justification, right or wrong, is a great motivator of people. Anyway, getting back to our case did you have any luck with Frank?"

"Yes. Frank can meet with us on Monday at 7:30 at Smiley's, if that works for you?"

"Good. See you there."

CHAPTER 14

Smiley's Bar

I again arrived first and took up my usual position in a booth in the back. I saw Taylor and Frank come in together, or at least at the same time. They were directed to me by one of the waitresses.

I stood as they approached the table.

Taylor spoke, "Hi Professor Miller, this is Frank."

Speaking to both of them, I said, "Please call me Rick. I really hate being called Professor Miller." I was only a couple of years older than Frank.

I continued, "This must be Frank about whom I have heard so much."

"Must be." Frank replied.

I continued, "Taylor tells me that you were working in the Haven-Newton Police Department at the at the time that Tammy went missing."

"Yes. You could say that. I was so new to the department that I was barely allowed to even listen to conversations about the crime, much less help with it."

"I guess I can sort of see that. Law enforcement can be oddly competitive in some ways. Maybe the older guys didn't want a young guy solving a case that they could not solve."

"There was not much chance of that. There was very little evidence to go on. Someone was able to get into the house and take the little girl without anyone noticing. Whoever it was must have been a real pro. I was told that he left no fingerprints, no usable DNA, no clothing, and caused very little damage. The weather was dry, so there were almost no footprints outside."

"How was he able to get to the house with the guard gate and all." I asked.

"At that time, the subdivision was so new that the guard gate had not been completely set up or manned. Also, I heard that there was a private access road which leads down to the old highway which the fire department required when the subdivision was built as an alternate way of getting in and out. It's hard to get back there even just to take a look."

"I presume that there are no cameras back there?"

Frank added, "There are a couple of cameras back there and a few cameras around the main entrance. But the subdivision was so new at the time of the kidnapping that the cameras, though physically in place, were not up and running."

How is it that people were living there without cameras?"

"Very few of the homes were occupied at the time. Some of the homes were occupied by people working on the subdivision in its sales departments. The Fitzgerald family was allowed to live there because Mr. Fitzgerald was instrumental in getting the project built."

"I wonder when Mr. Fitzgerald developed the clout to push a major subdivision like this through? I thought he was just a local realtor." Frank replied only that he could not say.

"Did you hear anything about the crime scene? How they got into her room? If they tore anything? We heard that there were no fingerprints. I guess we presume that they were wearing gloves?"

Frank added, "They said that there was not enough for DNA for testing."

I added, "That may have been the case at the time, but now there is something called touch DNA. This allows law enforcement to remove samples from only a few cells that remain after a person has touched something. A special process called PCR is used. This process causes the DNA to make copies of itself.

"A machine is used to heat the DNA to 95 degrees centigrade, which is very hot. At this temperature, the DNA unzips into two separate strands. A builder enzyme is added to the mix. It uses the separate strands to make more DNA copies. As most enzymes are destroyed at this temperature, it is important to use a super heat resistant builder enzyme, such as the type that lives in hot spring water.

"According to the literature, skin cells are transferred all of the time. Touch DNA has been used on samples from all sorts of subjects ranging from car steering wheels to a person's clothing.

"If we can get some item of clothing or something which the kidnapper may have touched from the evidence locker, we might get some touch DNA."

"Much time has now passed. Everything I have heard is that the kidnapper was very careful and might not have left anything, even for touch DNA. This means that at some point we are going to have to follow the money, and we are going to have to go after any associations that may have existed."

I continued, "It seems to me that if someone is going to kidnap someone's daughter, he might want to know if the person has enough money to make a kidnapping worthwhile. In other words, he would have to know that the parents had enough money to pay the ransom

"It is, however, going to be very difficult to examine Mr. Fitzgerald's, or anyone else's financial records for that matter, without a court order, particularly after so many months have gone by, and the case has been effectively closed."

Frank replied, "Let me see about the evidence locker. But we are going to have to put our heads together about the financial records and personal associations."

I left Smiley's and went home in my car. Taylor and Frank were still in the bar. I presume that they left at some point. I don't know whether they left together, or even if they are romantically involved. Both are attractive, and Frank seems to have his head on straight.

We agreed to meet again on Wednesday.

CHAPTER 15

Seventh Day of Class

Today is the day for one of my favorite lectures, examining the financial interests of the founding fathers in connection with their new Constitution.

At the Constitutional Convention, there were 55 founders. Notable among them were James Madison, Benjamin Franklin, and George Washington. All of the founders represented the propertied upper class. Not one attendee represented the small farming or mechanical class.

Of the 55 founders approximately 40 held what was known then as public securities. A public security is a loan made to the government prior to the Constitution. Article VI provides that all debts contracted before the Constitution shall be valid against the United States under the Constitution.

There were 14 speculators in land. They were protected by Article IV. There were 24 money lenders. They were protected by Article I which provides that only gold and silver may act as legal tender.

The 11 founders with mercantile, manufacturing, and shipping interest were protected by Article I which provides that no duties may be charged by one State against another and that all duties charged to a foreign country will belong to the United States.

The 15 founders with slaves were protected by Article I, Section 9, which provides that slavery could not be prohibited by Congress prior to 1808.

So, I ask you: Was it a coincidence that the financial interests of the founders were protected by the new Constitution?

Or: Were the protections afforded by the new Constitution the typical protections one would expect to see in a governing document drafted during the 1780's, which coincidentally protected the financial interests of the founders?

Consider this: An argument could be made that the primary objective of the formation of our government under the Constitution was to protect the financial interests of the influential. This would include having the new federal government assume the debts of the States, having the new federal government make good on the public securities held by 44 of the 55 founders, and allowing the new federal government to collect 100 percent of the duties levied on foreign goods to the exclusion of all of the States.

One could make an even more interesting argument that there have actually been three Constitutions, the 1789 Constitution, the 1791 Constitution, and the 1868 Constitution. The 1789 Constitution was practically an emergency measure needed to correct the defects of the Articles of Confederation and necessary to protect the economic interests of the founders.

Though drafted in 1787, the 1789 Constitution was ratified by the ninth State in 1789, and as nine States were all that were necessary for ratification under Article VII, in 1789 the 1789 Constitution went into effect. All States ratified the 1789 Constitution by 1791.

The 1789 Constitution provides, among other things, that debts contracted prior to the Constitution would be valid against the combined States after the Constitution and that all duties collected from foreign countries would belong to the government of the combined States. For many of the founders, the 1789 Constitution was sufficient even without a Bill of Rights, as it was deemed to contain a sufficient number of safe-guards for a functioning government.

However, several States asked for a Bill of Rights, and the majority of the founders promised to deliver one. This promise was kept in 1791 during the Washington Administration, when the Bill of Rights was added.

With the addition of the Bill of Rights, we had the Constitution of 1791.

Looking through the Bill of Rights we see that under its terms the new Congress could make no laws respecting the establishment of a religion for the combined States, and could make no laws prohibiting free speech, a free press, peaceable assembly, or the petitioning of the government for the redress of grievances. Under the Bill of Rights, the new Congress could not require citizens to quarter soldiers in their homes or be denied a speedy trial or a trial by jury, under many circumstances.

If we examine the Bill of Rights and the Declaration of Independence, we see that by the Bill of Rights, the colonists wanted to prohibit the new federal government from perpetrating the same or similar transgressions that were perpetrated by England before the Revolution, including quartering soldiers, denial of a jury trial, etc.

It might be interesting to note that between the Constitution of 1791 and 1868, nearly 80 years, the Constitution was Amended only twice, once by the 11th Amendment and once by the 12th

Amendment. The 11th Amendment granted sovereign immunity to the States. The 12th Amendment separated the election of the President from the election of the Vice President.

As we see, after the 1789 and 1791 Constitutions, many years later, we have the third Constitution, the Constitution of 1868, which came about after the Civil War and the passage of the 14th Amendment.

The 14th Amendment provides, among other things, that no State shall deprive a citizen of due process or equal protection under the law.

Prior to the 14th Amendment, the rights set forth in the Bill of Rights restrained only the federal government and not the State governments. However, after the 14th Amendment, the rights contained in the Bill of Rights were extended to the States. This was done by defining due process as a right contained in the Bill of Rights.

When the 14th Amendment provided that people were entitled to due process, it meant that they were entitled to the protections set forth in the Bill of Rights against State action as well as federal action. The equal protection clause provides that everyone is entitled to equal protection under the law.

Presuming that we have three Constitutions, allow us to consider an interesting legal/historical question. When someone claims to be a constitutionalist to which Constitution is he referring?

Are the Constitutions of 1789 and 1791 basically conservative documents limiting the federal government from intervening in social matters traditionally left to the States?

Is the Constitution of 1868 a liberal document where the federal government may be called upon to intervene to prevent States from engaging in forms of discrimination ranging from school desegregation to gay marriage?

The Supreme Court case concerning gay marriage is instructive. The case is known as Obergefell v. Hodges. This case made gay marriage legal nationwide. The decision was a close one, 5 to 4.

The majority opinion was written by Justice Anthony Kennedy and was joined by Justices Breyer, Ginsburg, Kagan, and Sotomayor, the liberal branch of the Court.

Writing for the majority, Justice Kennedy argues that same sex marriages should be recognized, relying on the 14th Amendment. To deny same sex marriage would deny couples due process and equal protection of the law. These five Justices are looking to the 1868 Constitution with its 14th Amendment allowing the federal government to intervene in protecting what it deems to be rights guaranteed under the Constitution, as amended.

Chief Justice Roberts and the remaining three Justices, Scalia, Thomas, and Alito, each offer a dissenting opinion in which one or more of the other dissenters joined. In upholding a ban on gay marriage, the dissenting opinions offer such positions as the need to define marriage as being between one man and one woman, that a ban would not have been unconstitutional at the time of the enactment of the 14th Amendment, that same sex marriage allows judges to be guided by their personal views, and that the right to gay marriage is not a right deeply root in the nation's history and tradition.

The dissenters do not appear to distinguish between classes of people, as it is classes of people who are expressly protected by the 14th Amendment.

At least in my opinion, the 14th Amendment was just that, an Amendment to the Constitution of the United States and should be so enforced. Lincoln worked tirelessly to make freeing the slaves a Constitutional Amendment, the 13th Amendment, rather than allowing it to become just a law or Supreme Court decision because he knew that only a Constitutional Amendment would make it possible for the federal government to enforce the Amendment against the States.

Whether one agrees or disagrees, the 14th Amendment forever changed our nation into one in which the federal government may involve itself in matters that the founders might never have thought possible, including discrimination.

If one assert that he is a constitutionalist, to not be prepared to uphold due process and equal protection clauses for all groups means that he is not a constitutionalist at all.

The question of religion also brings into question the different Constitutions. The First Amendment provides that Congress shall make no laws respecting the establishment of religion. This is known as the Establishment Clause.

Before and after the 1789 and 1791 Constitutions, the colonies continued the historical practice of allowing the States to establish State-wide religions with several States doing so.

The practice of having established State-wide religions appears to have died out on its own during the beginning of the 19th Century.

After the enactment of the 14th Amendment the practice was ended as the First Amendment's prohibition against the establishment of a religion was expanded from applying only to the federal government to also applying to the State governments.

The process of defining the Due Process Clause of the 14th Amendment as a right included in the Bill of Rights is known as the Incorporation Doctrine. A right contained in the Bill of Rights is incorporated into the 14th Amendment.

I offer the above thinking to you. Be prepared for questions about these issues and more on your final exam.

It might be interesting to note that the Constitution was not ratified by the State Legislatures or by a popular vote. No. It was ratified by conventions of individuals convened in each State for the purpose of ratification, similar to the Electoral College.

Class ended, and the students filed out. Taylor, lingering, approached my desk. She said, "I take it that you don't subscribe to the 'coincidental' theory of history?"

I replied, "I could say the same thing about you. You don't seem to think that Tammy's kidnapping at the same time that her father came into money was a coincidence either."

"You're right about that. I've arranged for us to meet with Frank tomorrow evening. Can you make it?"

"Yes. I'll be there."

CHAPTER 16

Smiley's Bar

Again, I was seated at the back of the bar in a booth waiting for Taylor and Frank. They entered and came to my table, without a waitress or hostess.

I started, "Hi guys."

Both Taylor and Frank said hi and sat down. Pleasantries were exchanged.

I continued, "It seems as if we have gotten as far as learning that no one witnessed anyone entering the subdivision and that fingerprint evidence does not exist. DNA evidence, if any, was very limited. No one, to my knowledge, inspected the back entrance for tire tracks, etc. The video monitors were not yet operative, so there was no video evidence.

"We have no information as to whether dogs were used. We have no information as to whether anyone connected with the family or the crime received or paid any large sums of money around the time of the crime.

"What the heck was done to solve this crime. Was the lead detective still working? Why didn't the FBI do more? I realize that the police department is under staffed and not fully equipped for a complicated investigation, but why weren't other people brought in. Was it an ego thing?"

Frank replied, "Those are tough questions, and I am not certain whether any of them can be answered at this late date."

I came in with, "Maybe we are approaching it from the wrong angle."

"Maybe we should be asking ourselves who had the juice to get the interstate to run through Newton? Or who had the financial ability to build Haven Lakes? If we presume that Don Fitzgerald did not have this kind of pull, there must have been someone behind him. We should be asking ourselves is who could that be?

"I presume that the kidnappers would know or need to know who had the financial ability to pay a ransom. Did Mr. Fitzgerald have this ability or did he have a backer with money that the kidnappers were actually trying to reach?"

Frank came back with, "You're getting out of my wheel-house now Professor. I know a little bit about the crime and how it was handled, or mishandled. But I don't know about financial matters regarding a project the size of Haven Lakes."

"We need to do some research about who owned the property where Haven Lakes is now located and who persuaded the local government to route the interstate through Newton. Maybe Taylor can help me with some leg work to see if we can piece together what happened with those projects."

Taylor chimed in "I'm okay with that. Just let me know what we need."

"Also, we need to know a little more about the physical evidence and whether we can get it from the evidence locker. I hope Frank that you can help us there. We need some information about the property on which Haven Lakes was built and who had an interest in such a development and maybe further development."

Haven and Newton are virtually in the desert. Haven Lakes was subdivided from a large tract of land in a low foothill area, just over the hill from Haven. Once completed, it became a paved, irrigated, and gated oasis in the middle of, basically, nowhere.

Haven, on the other hand, was already fairly built up. It had that that older desert look with low buildings with flat roofs and much concrete block to help with air conditioning which was needed nine months of the year.

Sand could be seen surrounding the asphalt parking lots for motels and shops. The houses were a bit more organized with a rocky hillside ascending from the main road up into the desert.

Newton was fairly low in the valley on the other side of the hill. It was a good area for citrus, and many of the properties had orange groves. Most of the properties were working farms, including my family property, which I inherited when my mom passed, just a year ago.

I was living at the family home while teaching at the junior college. I would probably have to sell because the orange crops over the past few years were not great, and my parents owed quite a bit as they had to mortgage the farm to get enough money to live, particularly after my father became ill. I planned on selling in the spring. As farming in general has become more difficult, I presume that other small farms were in the same predicament.

It was odd to me that someone would go in and make a development such as Haven Lakes in the middle of the desert. Maybe something was going to move near Haven or Newton which might make the area more valuable, or maybe just the pressure of more people moving into the vicinity made development viable.

The real estate market had been good. Mr. Fitzgerald was given the listing for all of the properties in the development. I presume that he intended to make quite a bit of money selling the houses at the prices that they would fetch.

I was hoping to get some help with the leg work about the property from Taylor, as Frank has a full-time job, and I am teaching.

As Taylor is attractive and nicely proportioned, I figured that when she was sent off to the county seat, she would look equally good in business attire.

Though to me she seemed mature for her age, her presentation of herself to others might seem more youthful, particularly in light of the way she dressed and spoke most of the time.

I didn't know whether to counsel her to dress more conservatively and to pay a little more attention to her use of the language.

As she typically presented herself, she might not seem appealing to an older, more mature woman, the type who might work in a government office in the county seat. Her looks might even be a little threatening to an older woman. I thought that perhaps some suggestions might be helpful, but I didn't know how well she would take it.

My plan was to ask her to go to the county seat in Bryan and see if she could find out more about the Haven Lakes property, and if there were any plans for more development in the area.

Now that the interstate was completed, Newton became just a short drive to the south entrance to Rock Ridge National Park. With better accessibility provided by the completed interstate, real estate in that area could become valuable as a tourist destination. Rock Ridge was a very popular place to visit, but before the road was completed, it was very difficult to reach by car, at least at the south entrance near Newton. Only the north entrance, which was pretty far away, was used in those days.

I asked, "Taylor, do you think you could go to Bryan and look up some information about the Haven Lakes property and nose around to see if there is any planned development in the area?"

"Sure. Sounds great. Anything to help the cause. But we have class tomorrow, and I will need at least two or three days in Bryan."

"No worries. We can have class tomorrow, and I will cancel class for Tuesday. That way you can leave early Monday and be in Bryan Monday, Tuesday, and Wednesday, and come back to debrief me and Frank on Wednesday evening. Early in the week will probably work better anyway as government offices are less likely to be closed."

"Good. I will plan on leaving early Monday."

We all left Smiley's. I went home in my car, and Taylor and Frank went home in their respective cars.

CHAPTER 17

Next Day, Eighth Day of Class

We went over how the powers granted to the new government in the original 1789 Constitution were not overly extensive. I told the class that the power of the federal government would be expanded as the country became more involved in foreign affairs and wars.

At the end of class, I advised the students that our Tuesday session for next week would be cancelled due to a personal matter and that we would meet again next Thursday.

Students began filing out of the classroom. When the classroom was empty, Taylor came over to my desk.

Taylor said, "I will be ready to go to Bryan early Monday. I've arranged to stay with my mom's cousin. She lives in Bryan near the Bryan City Hall which also houses the courthouse and the recorder's office. The two places I need to visit while I am there.

"I plan on staying Monday and Tuesday and returning on Wednesday. Thank you for canceling class on Tuesday."

Taylor left. I felt a little odd about not going to Bryan myself or at least not going with her. I guess that if she can't get anything done, I can always go later. With her innocent looks, she might do better than I would anyway. Taylor was scheduled to go to Bryan on Monday and to return on Wednesday. I suggested that we meet at Smiley's with Frank on Wednesday evening.

CHAPTER 18

Taylor's Return from Bryan

Though Taylor was scheduled to be in Bryan until Wednesday, as it worked out, she finished a day early. Rather than staying in Bryan, she returned home late Tuesday. She caught me at my office during the day on Wednesday, and we agreed to meet that evening with Frank at Smiley's Bar, as we had planned.

7:30 came around, and we all met at Smiley's. Taylor kept me and Frank spellbound with her story about her trip to Bryan.

She related her story as follows:

I left for Bryan on Monday morning. I got off to a little later start than I hoped. My mom had a couple of things for me to do first. Also, I needed to figure out what to take in the way of clothes. I still hadn't decided which back story I might use, and I would need a different outfit for each.

I thought that I might say that I work in a real estate office or was a teacher's assistant. Either could be easily checked. Also, either one would require a very conservative wardrobe.

I could say that I was a college student doing research, which was pretty close to the truth. Also, it would be easier to dress the part. I chose college student.

With the completion of the interstate, the drive from Newton, through the pass, through Haven, and onto Bryan was now about

45 minutes shorter. The entire drive could be made, with no traffic, in about 90 minutes.

I took off at around 10:30 which put me in Bryan at noon. My first stop was City Hall. The records department and the office of the County Recorder were both located there, as were the court rooms and court support offices.

The building is a one-story concrete block structure with a flat roof. The building is u shaped with a wide flat roofed portico over the outside entry area between the two wings. At the rear of the portico, there are large glass entry doors with fixed glass panes on either side of the doors. The fixed glass extended to the edge of each wing of the building.

Behind the entry doors and fixed glass there is a common hallway leading to the various offices and courtrooms located on either side of the building.

The floor of the common hallway is polished marble, not uncommon for a public building, with solid benches built in against the walls. I presumed that many cases were settled in this hall.

It was lunch time. Most public buildings such as this, I was told, are dark between 12 and 1:30 for lunch.

As it was hot outside, a few stragglers were still in the building. A sign pointed to the office of the County Recorder, my destination. I followed the sign to the particular office and found it to be closed, as I expected.

It was now about 12:45. I figured I'd wait in the hall for the office to open. I noticed an older gentleman on the other side of the hall. The couple of other older people with whom he was speaking left and exited from the building, leaving him alone.

He came over to me and asked what I was doing. I told him that I was a college student writing a term paper about land use for my environmental studies class. I asked him his name which he said was Wilfred Gordon. He said that people called him "Fred."

I asked him what he did, and he said he was retired and had become court-watcher. He described a court watcher as someone who hung around City Hall and watched notable trials and picked up any other interesting information from the recorder's office or the Planning Department, both of which were in the building.

He was not tall, maybe 5 foot, 7 inches. He was pleasantly plump around the middle. His hair was grey and curly. He reached out and shook my hand. His hands were strong and rough, as if he had used them to do real work for a long, long time.

He said that he had been a plumber for 50 years but that at 70, the work had become too physical for him. He said that he retired, and after trying a few new jobs, he resigned himself to court watching. He said that he had made several friends all of whom were around the courthouse almost every day. He was now 80.

He had a direct countenance. The type of person that one could trust. No airs. Also, he had no reason to be anything but truthful with me, as I appeared to have no stake in anything going on around the courthouse. I wished that I could have been as truthful with him.

I told him that the paper was about how changes in the desert could affect local wildlife and that one way to combat this was to require developers to make provisions for wildlife preserves as part of their development plan.

He asked if I had any particular development in mind. Not knowing what developments were being planned, the only name I could come up with was Haven Lakes.

He said that he was pretty sure that the Haven Lakes development was completed and that it did not include any provisions for the local wildlife. I told him that I knew that it was completed but that I was interested in finding out about the planning process and what was done to push it through the City Council and Planning Department.

Fred looked hard at me. He was visibly shaken. He said to me young lady I know that you are well intentioned, but you might be getting in a little over your head here.

I didn't really understand, but played along. I asked him why. He said that many strings were pulled to get Haven Lakes built. There were flood-plain and erosion issues. There were issues with the sewer. There were issues concerning how the streets and other utilities would be positioned. Environment groups protested vehemently about the lack of any plan to preserve the local wildlife. There were no provisions for schools or parks. But somehow, it got through.

He said the rumor around City Hall was that a mafia-type by the name of Antony Carbone was behind the development. It was thought that the plan for such a development would make more necessary the completion of the interstate highway from Haven to Newton which seemed, for some reason, to be of great interest to him.

I mentioned that I heard that Don Fitzgerald was involved. I explained that Mr. Fitzgerald had been a local realtor but that when the development was completed, he wound up with the largest and most expensive home in the subdivision and the exclusive right to sell all of the other homes.

Fred said that he had heard the same.

I asked him what he knew about Haven Lakes. He told me that he heard that Haven Lakes was only a minor part of a larger plan to build a very extensive development, including the largest casino and hotel complex in the State in Newton near the south entrance to Rock Ridge National Park.

He said that to get this done, the interstate would have to be completed through the pass between Haven and Newton in order to make the road from Haven and other parts of the State through Newton and to the south entrance to Rock Ridge Park adequate for his hotel and casino project. Otherwise, the hotel and the casino could not be built at all.

In the past, prior to the completion of the interstate, almost everyone accessed Rock Ridge Park through its north entrance, which is many miles away from its south entrance. This left the south entrance in Newton barely used.

Now with the newly constructed interstate, the south entrance would become the entrance of choice because it was actually closer and would become an easier drive from Haven, Bryan, and other parts of the State to the park.

If he could get the property around the south entrance, he could build a huge tourist hotel. Then all he would need would be a local Indian tribe with which to partner for the casino part of the project.

I told Fred I did not know much about casinos but that I was under the impression that in California, they could only be built by Indians on an Indian Reservation, and I did not think that there was a Reservation in the vicinity of the south entrance to Rock Ridge Park.

I could see Fred's eyes light up. He was going to have the opportunity to tell me everything he knew about the casino business. This fed directly into his first love - talking.

According to Fred, gambling was not an issue on Indian Reservations until 1979 when the Court ruled in favor of the Seminole tribe in Florida in connection with bingo on the Reservation. The Court decided that so long as bingo was not prohibited in the State, the State could not prohibit bingo on the Reservation.

In 1986, the court decided a case in California concerning the Cabazon tribe in which it essentially held that a tribe may conduct gambling activities on its reservation so long as the State also permitted those activities elsewhere in the State.

As this left the tribes free to establish gaming operations of all sorts in many States, Congress enacted the Indian Gaming Regulatory Act in 1988. The act broke down gaming into three classes including: Class I - social games for minimal prizes; Class II - bingo and certain card games where players were playing against one another; and Class III - games of chance or slot machines where players were playing against the casino or the house.

Class I games were regulated by the tribes. Class II games were regulated by the tribes and the State, but primarily by the tribes. Class III games were regulated by joint tribal/State compacts. Class III games were the most valuable to the tribes and were the most regulated. They were also the most valuable to the casino operation.

The Act confirmed to the tribes the exclusive right to regulate reservation gambling so long as the gambling activity did not violate federal or State law. Initially, in California, casino type gambling was considered illegal except on Indian Reservations.

Fred pointed out that for a guy like Carbone, it would probably not do him any good to manage a casino on an Indian Reservation because the location would not be sufficient to attract the type of clientele he needed.

Under the 1988 law, it became possible to build a casino off of a technical reservation. However, to do so, the Department of the Interior would have to take the land in trust and determine that a casino would be in the best interest of the tribe and the surrounding area, and the governor would have to concur. The only remaining question would be how far off of the reservation one could go.

Under the George W. Bush administration, the casino would have to be within commuting distance of a reservation. The Obama administration loosened the restriction so that it could be further away.

The land near the south entrance to Rock Ridge Park is very far from any Indian Reservation and would require heavy, if not impossible, negotiations to build.

Fred then asked me what I thought I might learn at the recorder's office. I said that I wanted to find out who owned the land where Haven Lakes was built to see if there was a connection with Mr. Fitzgerald.

After learning the existence of Mr. Carbone and the casino project, I thought it might also be a good idea to see how the casino project at the south entrance to Rock Ridge was progressing.

Fred looked at me inquisitively. Dear, you are a very nice girl, but I can tell you now that you are surely not going to get any of that information here. Anything of value about the Haven Lakes project or the proposed project at Rock Ridge Park is under strict lock and key. No one will be seeing that. Trust me. That information is too valuable.

So, I was in Bryan for less than two hours and have already been told that I will not be able to obtain that for which I was looking.

The lunch break was over. It was now getting onto 2 o'clock. Fred left. He said that he would be back the next day, which was Tuesday. Regardless of his admonition I decided to go to the recorder's office anyway.

The recorder's office was a typical sterile affair. The walls were a neutral light green. There was a long counter with individual windows. There was a rope indicating where one would stand in line. Outside of the immediate area of the windows and line, there were stand up type desks along the wall.

There was one person being served at window #2, and one person in line. The other four windows were closed. I waited behind the person in line. The gentleman at window #2 concluded his business, and the other person in line, a lady, went up to the window. I was next.

When she left, I went up to the window. There I encountered a woman in her fifties dressed in a conservative pants suit. I advised her that I wanted to find out who owned the property where the Haven Lakes development was located.

It was a slow day, and she was so kind as to explain how the ownership of the property had progressed, to the extent she could.

She said originally a sub divider owned the entire tract. The sub divider designed the streets and utilities and divided the land into residential lots facing the streets. There were other requirements such as setting aside land for a couple of small parks, the guard gate house, and an elementary school. The sub divider would build on some of the lots and sell the houses for his own account. He would also sell some of the lots to other builders who would build either for themselves or their clients.

She said that the public records would only show the name of the sub divider and the names of the people who bought either the finished houses or vacant lots.

She told me that the sub divider's name was a limited liability company, Haven Lakes LLC. She did not know the people behind the LLC.

I asked her whether I could get more information from the Planning Department. She said that she did not think so. She thought that a search with a title insurance company might produce more results.

The Planning Department was in the same building so I thought I might as well try there.

I arrived at the Planning Department around three. I met another woman there. She was younger and appeared college educated. She was well put together in a nice green dress with low black heals. She was appropriately made up and accessorized with jewelry.

I asked her about the Haven Lakes project. She told me that there were several sets of plans including plans for such things as grading, drainage, street design, utility locations, and lot lines. There were topographical maps. She told me that I could look over the plans in the office and advise her which, if any, of the plans I needed.

She would then contact the engineer or other person who produced those plans. She would need their permission to release copies as they were the technical owners. If they decided that they would release the plans, she would calculate the charges for each page. After paying, I could then receive the purchased pages. She said that it is possible that my request for plans could be denied altogether.

I had no idea which of the various plans would be of value so I told her that I would think about it and let her know. I left the office and the building. I drove out to my mom's cousin's house where I would be staying.

I arrived and knocked on the front door. She greeted me and let me into the house. She told me that she had her daughter's room ready for me. Her daughter was away at school. I put my few things in her daughter's room, freshened up, and met her downstairs in the dining room.

She made a nice dinner. After dinner, I was exhausted and went to bed. The next morning, I decided that I would return to City Hall and talk to Fred. Of all of the people to whom I spoke, he seemed to be not only the most genuine, but had the most useful information. He was such a decent man that I felt badly that I hadn't been completely honest with him about what I was actually doing in Bryan.

We had a nice breakfast, and I headed off to City Hall at 10. When I arrived, I saw Fred.

Fred asked if I went to the recorder's office or the Planning Department. I said that I had gone to both. He asked how it went. I told him that I basically got the run-around. He was not surprised, but neither was I.

He then asked me what exactly I was doing in Bryan. The time had come to tell him. I only hoped that telling him would not jeopardize our work.

I explained to Fred that a little girl for whom I used to babysit was kidnapped. I explained that no ransom demand had ever been made and that her body was never found.

I explained that the kidnapping took place months ago and that the case went cold after that time. The investigation was dropped. There was a funeral, which I attended. The little girl's mother was inconsolable and has been in a deep depression ever since.

I explained to Fred that I was not completely satisfied with the investigation so I decided to do some investigating on my own. I admitted that I learned almost nothing.

I explained to Fred that you came to my school as an adjunct professor to teach Constitutional Law. I told him that when you were introducing yourself, you explained that you were an attorney with the DA's office in Haven and worked with the criminal investigators as part of your job.

I told him that you seemed to be the closest thing to a real investigator that I might actually get to know. I also explained that I had a friend who was in the police department whose help I thought I could enlist.

I told him about our meetings at Smiley's Bar. I told him that you knew about DNA, phone records, and other such things. My deputy friend was a beginning deputy at the time of the kidnapping. Though his older and more seasoned colleagues kept him away from the actual investigation, he did hear and learn things which proved to be useful. Also, now, with a little more seasoning under his belt, he could be of much help, and he was.

I told him that we were all a little curious about why the back entrance to the subdivision had not been fully processed, why there was very little evidence of the physical break in, and why the video cameras in the subdivision were not operational.

Fred told me that he had heard about the very sad case of the kidnapping of Tammy Fitzgerald. He said that he was a little surprised that more was not reported. He chalked it up to the theory that maybe the police held back information from the press to see if some piece of evidence might show up that only the kidnapper would know. This could at least point them in a direction, right or wrong.

He then asked me an interesting question. He asked me why I was in Bryan looking at public records if I thought the little girl was kidnapped? Wouldn't my time be better spent looking for DNA or trying to find a witness?

I had to admit that I could see how he might feel that way. At that point, I guess I said out loud, for the first time, why we even cared about who developed Haven Lakes.

I told him that it seemed to me that a kidnapping was something typically done for money.

Tammy's father had obviously come into some money during the time the subdivision was being completed. He moved into the most expensive new house in the entire project. Even a not-so-clever kidnapper could figure out that he had money or at least knew people who had money.

Between his new-found prosperity and his association with Mr. Carbone, it seemed more reasonable that Mr. Fitzgerald could be seen as someone either with money or with access to someone with enough money to actually pay a ransom demand.

In short, I came to Bryan to find out from the public records whether Mr. Fitzgerald had money (which was unlikely) or had a benefactor (which was more likely).

Though I did not learn about a benefactor from the public records, I did learn about Mr. Carbone from you. So, I guess the trip was not a total waste of time.

I asked him if there was anything more he could tell me about Mr. Carbone. He told me that all of his information was strictly second-hand. He said that he heard that Mr. Carbone lived in a palatial compound in the hills north of the valley. The compound was heavily guarded, and no one, not even the authorities, were allowed in. The rumor was that trying to gain access could get someone killed.

They say that the compound is two miles up a long private driveway to the top of a hill overlooking the valley.

Fred said that Mr. Carbone was reputed to be very serious about his business dealings and really hated to lose, regardless of the fact that he did not need the money.

I thanked Fred profusely for all of the information he had given me. I apologized for not being completely forthcoming at first. He waived that off. He said that he was delighted that I finally trusted him and was happy to help.

I left City Hall and went back to my mother's cousin's house. It was now Tuesday afternoon. I was scheduled to stay over and come back on Wednesday, but I was anxious to get home and back to my own bed.

I left Bryan and returned to Newton Tuesday night. I had dinner and went to sleep. The next day I thought I might catch up with you at your office, and there you were.

I was first to comment, "Taylor, that was incredible. You learned more in a day and a half than all of the professionals who worked on this case learned in months. Interesting that the official channels gave you nothing but the run around, but you hung in and got some great information anyway.

"That Fred sounds like quite a guy."

Frank then threw in his observation, "I know that you guys are not in law enforcement on a full-time basis. That said, I know that the professor works with the DA's investigators on certain cases and that Taylor has some familiarity with this case because she knew the victim and worked for the family. But neither of you has really been in the trenches on a full- time basis as I have over the past couple of years.

"When you are working in a police station full time, not only are you investigating the cases assigned to you, but you are also hearing about all of the other cases which are assigned to other officers. One thing that strikes you is that either in the cases you are working on or the other cases coming into the office, you are constantly hearing about people doing or suspected of doing very bad things but against whom there is not enough evidence to charge them with a crime, or to even speak to them about a crime.

"These people remain just outside of the grasp of the system.

"These people don't seek notoriety. In fact, they go the other way. They stay hidden in the background. If someone should find out about them and bring them, or threaten to bring them, to the attention of the media, law enforcement passes them off as legitimate businesspeople who happened to be lucky enough to have made a great deal of money.

"The reason that they are not pursued by law enforcement is that either there is actually not enough evidence, that the evidence the police have is shaky, that the suspect's money and power would tip the scale away from a successful prosecution, or that the police have been paid off.

"These people live in palatial homes with high walls, electronic surveillance, and teams of armed guards. They claim that they need these precautions to protect themselves from criminals.

"This Antony Carbone is such a person. He is a really bad guy. So many stories have circulated around the station about this guy and all of the things he has done or been accused of doing. Some of the things are really frightening. But he is so well connected and has paid off so many people, that he has achieved an aura of respectability. He has made himself untouchable.

"Rumors have flown around about Carbone, including rumors that he has had people killed who crossed him on business deals.

"If he is planning to build a casino near the south entrance to Rock Ridge National Park, it is only a matter of time before it is done, regardless of who gets hurt, or worse, in the process."

I broke in, "Well Frank, it doesn't seem outside of the realm of possibility that the casino plan is a reality."

Turning back to Taylor and Frank, I tried to articulate what I was thinking.

"So here is what we know so far. A big hitter, this Mr. Carbone, wants to build a casino near the south entrance to Rock Ridge National Park. To do this, he first needs to extend the interstate highway through the hills that connect Haven to Newton. This accomplishes the result of connecting the interstate to the hotel and casino project which would be necessary to make that project possible.

"To get the interstate through, he would have to show a local need, other than his personal desire to build a hotel and casino.

"To do this, he knows or is told that he would have to build something that would benefit the community as a whole which would coincidentally require the interstate to be extended.

"Even with a plan as benign as a housing subdivision, he learns that the City Council and Planning Department would never approve such a plan for a complete outsider, particularly a reputed criminal.

"To this end, he enlists the services of Don Fitzgerald, a well-known local who he believes can be persuaded to cut a few corners, to act as his front-man.

"The first phase of the plan works brilliantly. The subdivision is planned, the interstate is completed which makes the subdivision possible, and the subdivision is built, even though a few corners are cut.

"The next phase of the plan is to get the Department of the Interior and the Governor on board to allow the casino to be built off of the reservation, as they say. This part of the plan becomes substantially more difficult.

"His boy, Don Fitzgerald, was fine for the local yokels at the City Council and Planning Department. Don knew these people from his years scraping buy as a real estate salesperson. Their wives and children are friends. They serve on volunteer boards and charities. They are members of the same private golf club. But Don never achieved any real success, at least the kind of success he thought he should have, until he was presented with the Haven Lakes project. Unfortunately for Don, when it came to the Department of the Interior and the Governor's office, he not only lacked clout, but he had no clout at all. To say that this displeased Mr. Carbone considerably might be one of the most egregious understatements ever uttered.

"So here is what we have. We have a kidnapping with no ransom demand and no body. We know that it is possible for a person to be kidnapped with no ransom demand so the kidnapper can exert power over a person, sexual or otherwise, or over a person in his or her orbit. As I told you guys before this happened to someone I knew. However, in that case the body was found, and the young lady who was kidnapped was of an age and appearance that could make her a more likely object of such a crime. Here we have a little girl.

"At the time of Tammy's kidnapping her father may have been involved with a gangster.

"Did the gangster have Tammy kidnapped to exert pressure on Don to get the hotel and casino project approved?

"Quite a few coincidences. But before going down that path, for which we have no evidence, except the statements of Fred, we might explore other available evidence. That would make the next step obtaining the evidence from the evidence locker and trying some more advanced DNA testing techniques.

"At this point, we have to presume that the physical evidence of the break-in into Tammy's room is now lost and that the rear entry into the subdivision has been compromised by the passage of time.

"Frank, do you think you can help us with the evidence locker? Also, do you think you can get some of the internal reporting about the crime which may not have been made public?"

Frank replies, "I'm pretty sure that I can get the evidence in the evidence locker. As to the internal reports, this might prove to be more difficult. At the time, I thought that the work of the lead detective was a little light, if you know what I mean. He was just a couple of weeks away from retirement, and between him and the other people working the case, they seemed to want to wrap it up. As a result, the reporting was not extensive or, at least, was not available.

"Also, and this might sound a little strange, the victim's family, particularly the father, was not pressing all that hard for results. Particularly with kidnappings, under most circumstances, the victim's family is all over the detectives. The family, as much as anyone else, often drives the investigation. The investigators take their cue from the family.

I responded, "Well, let's get the available physical evidence first and run DNA. After that, we can look into the investigation."

We just finished a record long meeting at Smiley's.

CHAPTER 19

Thursday, Ninth Day of Class

In today's class, we will consider the Electoral College. Article II of the Constitution states that each State shall appoint as many electors as it has Senators and Representatives. It goes on to state that the electors shall meet in their respective States and vote by ballot.

Under Article II, the person with the most votes would become President, and the person with the second most votes would become Vice President. This was changed by the 12th Amendment. The 12th Amendment requires two separate ballots, one for President, and one for Vice President. In this way, the President and the Vice President would be from the same political party. (Remember, there were no political parties at the time of the enactment of the Constitution.)

Notwithstanding Article II and the 12th Amendment, with our present Presidential election system, a State-wide popular election is held in each State, and a winner is proclaimed. With the exception of two States, 100 percent of the electors are required to vote for the winner of this State-wide election, even if that win is by a narrow majority.

So, I ask you, which is it? Does each elector vote for the candidate of his or her choosing or is each elector required to vote for the winner of the State-wide popular election? Under our present system, (with the exception of two States) each elector is required to vote for the winner of the State-wide popular election.

It is interesting to note that Constitutional scholars and the general public alike consider the founding fathers to have been among the most brilliant people to ever live. To that end, over the years, every word of the Constitution has been parsed and strictly construed.

So, when the Constitution states that the electors shall meet and vote, the present-day meaning is not that they are voting for a candidate of their choice but that they are voting for the winner of a State-wide popular vote.

This means that the founding fathers would be considered extremely intelligent and more than able to express themselves precisely in every area of law and government known to mankind, EXCEPT IN THE CASE OF THE ELECTION FOR PRESIDENT.

With the election for President, the phrase "meet and vote" does not mean that the electors would meet and vote for the candidate of their own choosing but would mean that they would meet and vote for the winner of a State-wide popular election.

Each elector does not vote but merely carries a piece of paper with a name on it determined by someone else. He then delivers that piece of paper to the Vice-President as his vote. Further, with the exception of two States, the winner of the State-wide popular vote receives 100 percent of the electoral votes of that State rather than a number of electoral votes proportionate to his number of votes.

This process greatly increases the possibility for a minority President, that is, a President who is elected after receiving fewer than a majority of the nation-wide popular vote but a majority of the electoral votes. This has been the case in two of the past four elections. Is this the result we, as a nation, want?

In Federalist 68, Alexander Hamilton, when approving the Constitution's method of Presidential voting, states that the electors are selected from their fellow citizens from the general mass and will likely possess the information and discernment requisite to such a complicated investigation as voting for President.

In my reading, Hamilton presumes that the electors themselves would be voting for the candidate as only they would possess the information requisite for such a complicated investigation. But that would prove to not be the case. The electors do not vote but only carry the results of a State-wide election to the Vice-President.

Perhaps it is time to amend the Constitution to reflect the way the election process is actually carried out. At the same time term limits for Congress should also be considered because holding office for 20 or 30 years affords a greater ability to sell influence to outsiders than would be afforded to someone with a limited term.

You might expect questions such as these on your final. The students appeared un-moved.

Class was over. The students filed out of the room. Taylor lagged behind.

I started, "That was quite a productive meeting we had on Wednesday. I am hoping to receive the physical evidence from Frank today. I'll send it along for DNA testing. When the results come in, we can plan our next meeting."

She replied, "That's fine. Should we wait to go over the questions of the investigation in general. Though I was never certain why, I am not surprised to hear that the investigation was not pressed as hard as it might have been."

"We can meet about the investigation any time you and Frank wish. My thinking was that the results of the DNA testing might narrow things a little so it might be a good idea to start there."

"Okay," she said.

Taylor left the classroom and went on about her business. I told her that because the testing would be done off hours by someone that I know that it might take less time to get the results than if the testing were done by a stranger. We would meet the night I receive them.

CHAPTER 20
DNA Testing

Frank was able to get the articles from the evidence locker to me later that afternoon. He brought them to my mom's house, where I was living.

We looked over the items. There were two stuffed dolls with which we presumed Tammy was sleeping. There were sheets, a blanket, and a bed spread, which we presumed was the bedding on her bed. There was a tiny piece of a torn shirt on the window frame which we presumed could belong to the kidnapper. Taylor added that Tammy's favorite teddy bear was not among the items.

"Isn't the DNA evidence kind of old at this point?" Frank asked. "It's been several months."

I replied, "I don't think so, but I am sure I will find out."

I took the evidence to the DNA lab on Sunday when the lab was closed for regular business. The lab is located in Bryan. I really did not want to advertise what I was doing so I avoided Haven. Also, Haven's lab might not be advanced enough for the small samples that I had.

I understood from Frank that when they tried to do DNA testing in Haven right after the kidnapping, it was said that there was not enough DNA for testing, and the matter was dropped.

In Bryan, I met with my contact, a fellow named Chad Davis. He was referred to me by Daryl Peters, one of the investigators with whom I worked when I was in the DA's office. Chad was an affable fellow. We met in his office. I brought the articles for testing.

I explained to Chad that DNA testing was tried but failed. The lab said that there was not enough material to test. Chad said that he has heard that complaint many times before. He said that new techniques were developed to test smaller samples.

Chad said that there is a new technique called touch DNA where the police remove samples of only the few cells that remain after a person has touched something such as clothing. He said that as humans, we shed an enormous number of skin cells each day, and these cells are transferred to clothing and other objects.

Chad said that he intended to harvest DNA by swabbing, scraping, and using tape to lift cells from fabric or even a piece of clothing.

A process known as PCR would be used to process the DNA sample, provided that a sample is available.

To carry out PCR, a machine is used to heat the DNA to 95 degrees centigrade. At this temperature, the DNA unzips into separate strands. From the strands, a builder enzyme is used to make more DNA copies. As most enzymes are destroyed at this temperature, the key to PCR is to use a heat-resistant builder enzyme. This builder enzyme is a bacterium that lives in hot water springs that may survive in the high temperature environments.

During PCR, the builder enzyme causes the DNA to copy itself millions of times; this allows scientists to obtain plenty of DNA from a few cells in under an hour.

I felt good about leaving the samples with Chad. At this point, he was so removed by distance and time from the original crime that it would be unlikely that anyone would think to question his testing. Also, as a scientist, he seemed above the fray of the investigation and its outcome, as law enforcement might be. Additionally, he seemed to know what he was doing.

Late Sunday evening, I returned to my mom's home in Newton from Bryan. I caught up with Taylor at my office on Monday.

CHAPTER 21

Tenth Day of Class

Class met on Tuesday. This would be the last class before the final exam. We did an extensive review.

I knew that not much would be remembered from a survey class. I hoped that the basic rights preserved in the original Constitution and the Bill of Rights, however, would be.

I hoped that the students would remember that initially the Bill of Rights was designed to apply only to the federal government. After the Civil War, the 14th Amendment would be used to apply the Bill of Rights to the States. This would be done by defining due process as a denial of a right guaranteed by the Bill of Rights.

I thought that the economic reasons for the Constitution in the first place were of interest, including the ability to tax, the exclusive right of the federal government to levy duties on foreign countries, the creation of a common market among the States by prohibiting one State from imposing duties on another State, and the assumption of the debts of the various States by the United States. The Electoral College was of some interest, as they would be voting in the near future.

To me, the overriding principal that I tried to instill was not necessarily being right, but to marshal facts to support one's conclusions. Were the economic interests of the founders a coincidence? If so, tell me why?

I announced to the class, "Everyone, we will skip the next class so that you can study for the final exam." A student asked if it would be multiple choice or essay. I told the class that it would be multiple choice.

The students filed out of class as usual. Taylor lingered, as she often did.

I said, "I plan on having the results from the DNA testing on Thursday. I could meet Thursday evening."

"Smiley's at 7:30?" she replied.

"Yes."

CHAPTER 22
DNA Results

Taylor, Frank, and I were seated in our usual booth in the back.

I started, "I have the DNA results."

I opened a large envelope that contained a two-page document. The document started with the usual disclaimers about what you might and might not determine from DNA testing.

We were not interested in the health issues, if any, of the test subject. We were only really interested in establishing identity.

I started, "The DNA results were compared to that of all of the subjects from whom DNA was taken. This included, of course, Tammy's father, mother, brother, you, the housekeeper, the guards, a couple of delivery people, several relatives, and everyone else around Newton and Haven who volunteered DNA for this test or who were tested for other reasons.

"There were no hits with the DNA on file. That means that the father was not in her room on the night of the kidnapping or even around that time."

"Does that mean that he did not do it?" Taylor asked.

"It means that it does not appear as if he personally went into her room and did it. It does not mean that he could not have had it done by someone else."

Frank interjected, "My recollection is that DNA was taken from several people, in addition to the family. The family, particularly the father, was quite anxious to give a sample. The ease with which the DNA was collected implies to me that the providers were pretty certain that it would not be their DNA."

Looking at the test results, I continued, "The DNA results showed that the subject was a man, possibly of Latin descent whose DNA was not taken during the investigation. No identification from DNA appears possible, at this time."

Frank concluded, "I guess that puts us back to square one."

I replied, "Not really. It shows that no one from the family personally went into Tammy's room to grab her, and that it was someone from the outside acting on his own or who was hired to do the job.

"If the kidnapping was not a random act done to hold someone for a few days, there could be a money trail, as would be necessary for one person to hire another to do such a job."

Taylor asked, "How are we going to get access to financial records? We are not the police, at least officially. We do not have a pending lawsuit."

I asked, "How about the detectives who worked on the case originally?"

Frank replied, "The primary detective retired from the force and would probably be of little help. He might be worth contacting, but judging from the way the case was handled at the time, I doubt that he would be of much use."

I started, "Here is what we know and don't know. There is no video of the area where the kidnapping took place. The DNA shows that a man took her, but does not show the man's identity, as his DNA is not on file.

"There was no ransom demand. At 12, Tammy might not be the target of a random kidnapping for sex, though we have no way of knowing whether we are dealing with a psychopath who is into that sort of thing. If this were the case, one would think that a body might turn up.

"The police investigation at the time appears to have been less than perfect. This might be chalked up to the lead investigator's pending retirement. Perhaps he was paid off or threatened. Perhaps he just wasn't very good. Under any of those circumstances, there would be no reason for him to speak with us now. To do so, he would either be confirming his incompetence or admitting to a payoff or conspiracy. Our only hope here would be a crisis of conscience, which is not likely.

"One would hope that a truly caring father might be able to extract this information by force. Another thing that has not happened.

"Tammy's father was reputed to be involved with a gangster, Antony Carbone, around this time. It appears as if he was able to come through with permission to build Haven Lakes and to complete the interstate. However, as far as being able to do anything with respect to obtaining permission to build an Indian casino, this appears to have been beyond his capabilities. The site is technically too far from an Indian Reservation to be a location for gambling. Could this be a coincidence? Or could Carbone be flexing his muscles.

"So, we ask ourselves, how do we proceed? It appears possible that we could arrange to speak with the lead investigator. However, speaking to the lead investigator would likely result in nothing more than a litany of denials and lies.

"This leaves only the most difficult and dangerous avenue – investigating Mr. Carbone."

Taylor injected, "Yes, that would be difficult and dangerous."

Taylor continued, "According to Fred, Mr. Carbone lives in a complex on the top of a hill accessible by one long and winding driveway, or from air by helicopter. A helicopter would be the way to go, but we could never sneak in that way.

"This leaves hiking in to get a look, which could get us killed, or coming up with a ruse, such as pretending to be from the health department or the building department."

I chimed in, "How about a drone?"

I continued, "We could get a drone with a high-powered camera, and see if we could get a look. At this time, drones are so rarely used that they might not expect it. It is, of course, possible that a drone would be shot out of the sky, but at least no one would die, at least at that time. If he found out who sent the drone, things would get rough."

Frank weighed in, "I guess the drone would be the place to start. It's the safest of several unsafe ideas."

Taylor asked Frank, "What have you heard about Carbone's place?"

"According to everyone on the force, it cannot be penetrated. There is a long, exposed driveway up to the house. There are guards at a guardhouse and roving around the grounds. There is an electric fence around the whole place. Besides, we wouldn't know where to even start to look."

Taylor then asked, "What will we learn from seeing the compound? Even if we were given full run of the place, we would not know where or for what we are looking. I say we try the retired detective and see what he knows."

We all agreed that we had much to consider. We left Smiley's. I, for one, went home.

CHAPTER 23
Final Exam

I administered the final exam as scheduled. After class, the students filed out as usual. Also, as usual, Taylor lingered behind.

Taylor said, "That exam was pretty hard,"

"I hope you were not expecting a softball," I replied.

She came back with, "Now that the final is over, you are no longer my teacher. Since I am 19, I guess that means that we are just two adults."

"I guess you're right."

For the several weeks I had known her, I tried my hardest to keep things professional, or at least student-teacher like. I was obviously attracted to her. She was 19 and a full-grown woman, and a beautiful one at that.

It's odd that in our culture a student, even one over the age of consent, is considered a child and not suitable for socializing. It would have been much easier if I had not been her teacher.

Unfortunately, over the weeks, I came to appreciate more about Taylor Shaw than just her looks. She had a certain depth of character that was even more impressive than her appearance.

She was intensely loyal. She learned how to run the farm to take care of herself and her mother. She put up with her mother's drinking and "gentlemen" friends. She helped out Moose and Carol and their friends, even when she was doing without. She passed on having a social life with her classmates.

Loyal to a fault. She would not accept that the kidnapping of Tammy would go unsolved, if she had anything to do with it. Her lack of self-interest, as well as her persistence, were very provocative, at least to me.

I, on the other hand, could be seen as being involved so that I could be close to her. So that I could get to know her. So that I could become romantically involved with her. Ideals not nearly as lofty as hers. I cannot say for certain that these were the only feelings that drove me, but I also cannot say that they were not part of the equation.

As a result, I was very careful to maintain a friendly relationship with no overtures of romance. Partly because it was the right thing to do, and partly because if she was not interested, my feelings would have an escape route, albeit a small one.

I could not imagine that anything would stop her now. She was her own force of nature. Too bad for me.

She said, "Now that you are no longer my teacher, can we go out?"

"You mean like a date?"

"Of course."

"Don't you think that could be a little dangerous? It could tear us away from our quest to find Tammy's kidnapper."

"It might, but not by much," she replied.

It was final exam week, and the parking lot was nearly empty. I had been walking Taylor to her car while having this discussion. We arrived at her green truck. She turned to face me. There was very little space between us. With her back against the door, she turned and looked directly at me. She drew closer. She kissed me hard on the lips. I kissed back. We just had our first kiss.

I have to admit that it felt very good and broke some of the tension between us.

She opened the door and positioned herself in the driver's seat. She started the truck and slowly pulled away.

As the truck began to pull away, I could see her through the glass window behind the driver's seat. All I could think about was every song that I ever heard about the feelings that someone has when the person he cares most about leaves without things between them being settled.

She went home.

We agreed to meet with Frank at Smiley's on Wednesday after her last final.

CHAPTER 24

Do We Interview the Detective?

On Wednesday after Taylor's last final, we all met at the same booth at the back of the bar. We went over the idea of flying a drone over the Carbone complex to get a look. Everyone agreed that it would be better to use a drone than to try to hike in, at least for now.

"What information do you guys think we will get from seeing the complex?" Taylor asked.

I replied, "I don't know if we will get any information about the kidnapping, but we will at least learn the scope of the property if we need to get in there at some point"

Taylor went on, "I agree with that, but I think we should try to talk to the lead detective on the case. We might learn what was done and what was not done. Much more may have been done than we think."

Frank added, "Remember, I am only working from my recollection from many months ago. I was brand new on the job, and all of the things that were investigated were not shared with the department in general, or with me in particular. I think it is a good idea. I would say that it would be better if just the two of you went. Knowing that I am with the department might make him less forthcoming, and it would not help me keep my job either."

We all agreed. Taylor and I would arrange a time to interview Detective Pratt, if he would see us, at his home in Mount Shasta. Mount Shasta was about 500 miles away, an approximately six-hour drive, given the condition of the mountain roads.

We agreed that we would drive up, get a motel room, stay the night, and see Detective Pratt the next day, in the morning. The drive was a little too long to drive up, get an interview, and drive back on the same day.

We were both finished with school for the semester. Only Frank had to work.

CHAPTER 25

The Trip to Mount Shasta

I telephoned Detective Pratt and arranged for me and Taylor to meet with him on Saturday morning. Taylor and I would drive up, stay the night, and have plenty of time to meet with him. To his day, I have no idea why he would accept such a meeting. It would seem that the Tammy Fitzgerald case was clearly not his most brilliant police work, and he would only be subjecting himself to less than terrific reviews.

I booked two rooms in a motel in town. It was the one with the largest ad and, from the map, appeared to be fairly close to Detective Pratt's home.

Taylor and I took off in my car on Friday at 11 in the morning. I expected that we would arrive at the motel in the early evening, around 6, depending on the conditions, the traffic, and the number of stops.

I thought that the drive would do us good. We would have an opportunity to talk about the case and the direction it might take.

I picked up Taylor outside of her mother's house in Newton. We took a couple of surface streets until we entered the interstate. The interstate, having recently been finished, was wide open, particularly on the newer section between Newton and Haven. The original part in Haven and to the west was fair, but not like the new section.

We would be driving west from Newton through Haven, and then through several cities and towns to the west of Haven before taking a cut off to the mountain road leading to Mount Shasta. The south entrance to Rock Ridge National Park was to the east of Newton, the opposite direction from Mount Shasta and other populated areas along the original interstate.

Taylor started, "I want you to know that I really enjoyed your class on the Constitution. The final was very hard, but seemed fair."

I replied, "Don't worry, you did very well. You were one of my best students."

"Most history classes treat the Founding Fathers as saints doing altruistic work. You showed us what they did, and some of their motivations, allowing us to draw our own conclusions.

"The financial motivation was particularly interesting. I found interesting the fact that the founders were not only looking to establish a form of government but were also looking to solve some of the financial problems that existed under the Articles of Confederation.

"I thought that looking at the economic interests of the participants at the convention was enlightening.

"A significant group favored a new, stronger central government to take over the debts of the States, rather than go bankrupt.

"A group had mercantile and shipping interests which would benefit from duties on foreign goods, and these duties could be used to finance the new government.

"A group owned slaves and had an interest in not having that horrible practice outlawed, at least right away. Its survival was kicked down the road to 1808, 20 years later, and mostly in the territories.

"Really interesting stuff. I guess the fact that the founders had an economic interest and some of those interests were solved or at least addressed in the Constitution could be viewed as more than a coincidence. But I got the feeling that you don't really subscribe to the coincidental theory of history.

"I would suspect, however, that many people would disagree with your interpretation, even though you seemingly just put the information out there and allow your students to draw their own conclusions.

"But implying reasons other than pure altruism when you're speaking about the Constitution is deemed sacrilegious in most circles."

This might be the longest that I have ever been silent in a discussion about history, particularly the history of the Constitution. Having said that, I felt that it was my obligation as a teacher and general blowhard to jump into the conversation.

To this end, I said, "The economic stuff was actually the work of a famous historian by the name of Charles A. Beard in the beginning of the 20th Century. Regarding your remarks about altruism, it is interesting to note that later in life, even Charles Beard changed some of his economic theories and returned to the theory that the Constitution was primarily a work of altruism, as you put it."

Our conversation then turned to the case of Tammy. Taylor, Frank, and I had been working on this case for a few weeks, and it seemed as if we knew at least as much about it as the local authorities.

I added, "With respect to our case, the coincidental theory of history might be interesting to explore.

"Let's see, at the time of the kidnapping, the subdivision was so new that it did not have working video cameras. The back way into the subdivision was considered too remote for use.

"Telephone records were virtually non-existent. During the time in which a relevant call would have been made, the mother and Jason made or received no calls. Mr. Fitzgerald made no calls, but did receive one call from his gardener.

"Mr. Fitzgerald worked for a gangster to build a lavish subdivision in virtually the middle of nowhere, at least partly to make necessary the construction of the interstate highway to provide access.

"This interstate highway would coincidentally connect the section of the highway coming from Haven and places to the west, through a lightly-traveled mountain pass between Haven and Newton, and east to the south entrance to a national park, which entrance was rarely used. The national park was almost always entered through its north entrance many miles away.

"The same gangster was rumored to be planning a large-scale hotel and casino project near the south entrance to the same national park, which, until the building of the interstate, was virtually inaccessible, or at least not comfortably accessible to tourists. The completion of the interstate through Newton would convert the south entrance from being almost never used to a significant tourist destination and, thereby, a valuable place for a hotel and casino.

"It was rumored that Mr. Fitzgerald was again working with the same gangster to get permission from the Department of the Interior and the Governor's office to partner with an Indian tribe to build a casino. The casino would be far from an Indian Reservation.

"Throughout the time that all of this work was being done for this reputed gangster, Mr. Fitzgerald's daughter is kidnapped.

"Many coincidences."

"I would have to agree," was Taylor's response.

We turned off of the interstate and were now on the mountain road to Mount Shasta. It was now around 5:30, and we were approaching the tiny town.

We found the motel. It was not lavish, but it looked clean. The building is two stories with stairs at each end of an outside walkway. The front windows looked onto the walkway, and the front doors opened onto the walkway. From the street, one could see the end of the building. The front door side could be seen from the parking lot.

At the rear of the property, a restaurant faced into the parking lot.

We parked in the parking area. I went to the office. I signed in, gave the man my credit card, and secured two room keys. He said that we would be in rooms 210 and 211. There was a door that connected the two rooms, but that door was usually left locked.

I asked him if there was a place to eat nearby. He said that the restaurant in the back of the parking lot was pretty good and, at this hour, would probably be my best bet.

I returned to the car and collected Taylor and the little bit of luggage we had. She followed me up the stairs and to room 210. I opened the door. The room was typical. The front door and window were on the walkway wall. The room heater and air conditioner were built into this wall below the window. The drapes were usually drawn so that people walking by could not see in.

At the back of the room, on one side, there was an open closet. On the other side, there was a bathroom with a toilet, a basin, and a shower over tub. There was soap, shampoo, and clean towels.

I told Taylor that I had rented this room for her and room 211, next door, for me, so she would have some privacy. The initial look of misunderstanding left her face.

I took my things and headed for room 211. I said that we could freshen up and meet back here for dinner in an hour. She seemed agreeable.

I entered room 211. It was exactly the same as room 210. I put my things away and took a shower. After showering, I got dressed and watched the news on television.

After the hour elapsed, I went back to room 210 to see how Taylor was doing, and whether she was ready for dinner. She was. She was a ready-to-go girl. She didn't spend a lot of time primping in front of a mirror or fussing about her clothes.

We walked to the restaurant at the back of the parking lot. One of the waitresses seated us by the window. There were only a couple of tables occupied. We ordered.

Taylor asked, "Do you think that we will be able to get any information from the detective tomorrow?"

I replied, "Truthfully, I doubt it. If he didn't or couldn't gather evidence at the time of the kidnapping, when he had access to the evidence, it is unlikely that he would know or reveal anything more now.

"As to our ability to obtain financial records now, since the Right to Financial Privacy Act in 1978 and similar laws enacted by most States, everyone knows that it is nearly impossible to obtain financial records without a subpoena or a warrant, even for law enforcement.

"But that being said, I do firmly believe that watching his demeanor while answering questions or just talking about the case should certainly be enough to make the trip worthwhile."

"How about financial records?" Taylor asked.

"The only person, other than the actual account owner, who can obtain financial records would be a bank employee, like a teller. Bank employees typically have access to records of their customers.

"But this access is closely monitored, and if an employee looked up the records of a customer, another bank employee overseeing that employee would find out, particularly if it happened on more than one occasion, and he would report it.

"Even if we found someone in Mr. Fitzgerald's bank who would give us his records, it is likely that we would get caught and would be in big trouble.

"But how important is that, really? Everyone already knows or at least highly suspects that Mr. Fitzgerald received compensation from Antony Carbone for the interstate and Haven Lakes projects. I mean, we know that Mr. Fitzgerald received something from somebody to enable him to buy the big house, or the house itself may have been the currency.

"In a perfect world, Fitzgerald would be paid off and then use those funds to buy his new house. The identity of the person paying him could then be established from the funds transfer. I really don't think that someone as savvy as Mr. Carbone would pay anyone in such a way that there would be a paper trail leading right back to him. Any compensation would be through multiple shell companies, would go to an offshore account, and would be virtually untraceable.

"Even if Mr. Fitzgerald was the receiver of a bribe or money to make bribes in the Haven Lakes case, would that have anything to do with the kidnapping?"

Taylor asked, "How about receiving something for the work to get an Indian casino at the new location?"

"I guess we have to presume that there would be money or some other form of remuneration involved, but does that get us closer to the kidnapper?

"If there was a ransom paid, we would know from the initial police investigation how that was accomplished and the source of the money, as the authorities would have had access to those records. We would know Mr. Fitzgerald received the money to meet the ransom demand.

"After thinking this stuff through, it dawns on me that it's the lack of a ransom demand, the lack of a ransom payment, and a great deal of inaction by the local police that might be the more interesting to consider."

Dinner was winding down. Taylor excused herself to use the bathroom. As she walked away, I was struck by just how beautiful she was becoming. Her depth of caring about her little charge and her thinking process heightened the physical attraction.

When I first saw her, I thought that she was just another teenager in my class. I initially thought that her need for a private meeting was overly dramatic.

I was pretty dismissive, and I have to confess that her youthful look and countenance turned out to be a distraction from substance, both from the substance of the crime and from her substance as a person.

I have always thought of myself as being enlightened, accepting all people regardless of race, age, gender, appearance, and disability. But it appears as if I have been quite wrong about myself for a very long time.

Taylor's age and looks tricked me, or at least distracted me from the real heart of the matter. A child had been taken, and it was the perseverance of another almost-child who would either find her or die trying; that was the central message here. Silly me for doubting her.

Taylor returned from the restroom. Together, we returned to her room. I said goodnight and retired to my room next door. Once there, I put on a pair of sweats and settled in to watch an hour of TV before bed. I fell asleep in front of the set around 9:30, which was my custom.

Bang! At 10:30 the house phone rang. The loud ring of a land line, among the few left, startled me. I practically jumped out of my skin. Who could that be? No one even knows that I am here, much less the telephone number of this place. I picked up the phone and said hello. The voice at the other end was Taylor's. She said that she could not sleep and asked me to come to her room.

I went next door to her room. She greeted me sitting on the edge of the bed. Without saying anything more she motioned for me to come over next to her. She stood up directly in front of me.

We were separated by only a few inches. She looked spectacularly beautiful. I looked deeply into her eyes. She moved a little closer and began to softly kiss me on the mouth.

She removed her shirt and bra still standing in front of me. She helped me off with my shirt. We gently embraced, exploring each other's bodies with our hands while gently kissing.

We sat down on the edge of the bed. We each undressed completely. We turned back to one another and continued kissing and exploring. Shortly after that moment, we became lovers. All of the emotion and feelings I had for her came flooding to the surface, heightening her touch and our lovemaking.

When we were through, without a word, we both fell asleep and woke up the next morning to tackle the next challenge in our series of challenges.

Upon awaking, I was able to muster, "Hi, my sweet."

"Hi." She replied.

I asked, "Shall we get breakfast?"

"Yes."

I returned to my room, took a quick shower, got dressed, and returned to her room. She was dressed and ready.

We went to the restaurant in the motel downstairs and ordered breakfast. It was 9 a.m.

"How far away is the detective's house?" she asked.

"About 20 minutes."

After breakfast, we got into my car and drove to the home of Detective Oliver Pratt.

Detective Pratt's home was modest but appeared comfortable. I parked on the street in front of the house. We exited from the car and headed towards the front door.

Detective Pratt came out of the house and said, "I've been expecting you."

We exchanged pleasantries. He invited us inside.

The inside of the home looked similar to the outside. Not lavish, but comfortable. With two overstuffed large chairs with ottomans, an overstuffed couch, end tables, a coffee table, and a modern-looking television set in the corner.

He sat in one of the chairs while Taylor and I shared the couch.

I started, "So, Detective Pratt, as you know, we are here to ask about the Tammy Fitzgerald kidnapping case."

"Please, call me Ollie. Everyone else does."

"Okay Ollie, what can you tell us about it?"

"That was a very difficult case. The child was taken in the early morning hours. The video cameras scheduled to be set up around the new subdivision had not yet been put in place.

"We never had a ransom demand, which we were expecting. We were working on the assumption that since Mr. Fitzgerald appeared to have a lot of money, judging from his new house, his daughter might become a target for kidnapping.

"By not having a ransom demand, we had no direct contact with a possible perpetrator, which we might otherwise have had. This left the suspect pool wide open. To us, it seemed so unlikely that someone would kidnap another person and not expect a pay day.

"This left us with the possibility that the girl was taken for some sick fantasy or just for kicks. I'm sure you know that there are cases like that. With no ransom demand, we had no real starting point or motive.

"We checked the Sex Offender Registry. We found a few offenders around the area. We interviewed all of them and their associates and got nothing. They all had airtight alibis.

"We comprehensively searched the area."

Taylor interrupted, "Sorry for interrupting. I don't know if you know that I was Tammy's babysitter just prior to her kidnapping. I live just over the hill in Newton. I kept up with the case best I could. I went to the funeral. I tried to console Tammy's mother, which did not go well. But I don't remember hearing about much of a search, and there were no reports that DNA testing was done, even though you guys had complete control of the room in which she slept."

Detective Pratt continued, "I think the department got a pretty bad rap. We did search. We were told that the DNA techniques available were not sufficient to test the small amounts of DNA that could be collected.

"Besides, we did not advertise the many steps we were taking."

Taylor would not be silenced. She went on, "How about phone records? How about financial records? Why was the investigation stopped after just a couple of months?"

Detective Pratt replied, "We checked the phone records for the entire family. Around the time of the event, there was only one call to or from a family member. It was an incoming call to Mr. Fitzgerald from his gardener. We didn't feel that gardening instructions would give us any useful information about a kidnapping.

"As to financial records, as there was no ransom paid, we didn't think that delving into financial records would be very productive. If a ransom had been paid, financial records might have been helpful in determining the recipient of the payment, a likely suspect.

"If a ransom had been paid, we might have checked Mr. Fitzgerald's financial records to see if he had an influx of cash which he might use to help him pay a ransom. Because no ransom was paid, we felt financial information was not important as it would not lead us to a recipient of a ransom or to someone helping Mr. Fitzgerald pay a ransom."

I asked, "Did the department ever investigate Mr. Fitzgerald's association with Antony Carbone, a known gangster?"

Detective Pratt answered, "My boss required all of us involved with the investigation to tread very lightly with respect to Mr. Carbone. We had no evidence linking him to the crime, and we did not want the press or the rumor mill to get involved. My boss felt that this would be unfair to him.

"Information was so tightly guarded that we were not allowed to share any information about the investigation with anyone, with even the junior members of the department."

I then asked, "Was this the reason that the investigation was cut short?" Without time to answer, Taylor broke in.

By this time, she was visibly agitated, and she would not be stopped. She interjected, "Frankly, Detective Pratt, your investigation was a joke. A perfunctory look at the Sex Offender Registry? A half-assed search of the area? No DNA testing?"

She went on, "No comprehensive examination of the financial records? Why, because there was no ransom demand, or because your boss did not want to inconvenience a known gangster? Sorry, but that all looks pretty bad to me."

Reeling, Detective Pratt replied, "Well, that was the best we could do, and after a few months our boss told us to close the case."

After this exchange, we tried to mend things with a few superficial pleasantries, but that was not to be. Communication had already broken down. We left the house, returned to the car, and drove away.

Once in the car, Taylor said sheepishly, "I'm so sorry about losing it in there. I just couldn't stand the BS, and it really irritated me. Sorry."

I replied, "No reason to apologize. I was equally pissed, and I am not nearly as invested in the case as you are."

It was now getting onto one o'clock. We had all of our stuff, and I had checked out of the motel. We figured we would make the drive back directly, as the worst part of the road would be the first part, which I hoped to tackle while it was still light.

I was a little sad that we could not stay longer after the really wonderful night we had the night before, but it was time to go back. Things were pretty quiet for the first couple of hours. I don't think that either of us was mad at the other, but we were each processing the morning, and perhaps the night before, separately.

Conversation would start again a couple of hours into our drive of several hours.

It's funny. As I said before, when I first met Taylor, I thought she was just another overly dramatic teenager. But as I got to know her better, I realized that she had quite a bit of depth. She had real concern for her mission. I thought that she was just pretty, and I was more than willing to help her out on that basis alone. But she surprised me with legitimate and complex feelings about the case, and she did all of this without much support from home. Shallow me.

With my mother getting sick and my moving back home to take care of her, I found myself without the personal resources to forge any kind of relationship with anyone, man or woman. The Taylor thing was just something I fell into by accident. I'm hoping that it will remain a good thing.

———

While we were driving back, and far out of our earshot, Detective Pratt called his former boss, Commissioner John Burrows, to tell him about the meeting.

Commissioner Burrows asked, "How did the meeting go with the professor and the girl?"

Detective Pratt replied, "It was all going pretty well with the professor. I thought that they would be easy to satisfy; then the girl jumped in.

"She is a real bitch. She jumped all over me and was not afraid to speak her mind. I thought she was going to kick my ass. Fortunately for us, they don't know anything, so all of her ranting and raving really didn't mean much.

"Their knowledge of investigatory procedures is so minimal that they wouldn't be able to find the kidnapper if he turned himself in and confessed while they were in the room."

Commissioner Burrows asked, "Did they say anything of interest?"

"No. They only complained about what a bad job we did. So, they know nothing."

"Okay, let me know if you hear from them again."

The telephone conversation between Pratt and Burrows ended as we continued our drive home in silence. I was waiting for her to break the ice.

She started, "What did you think of that guy?"

I replied, "Not much. How about you?"

She said, "He was either incompetent, involved, or both, probably both. You always know when someone is lying because he spends the entire conversation making excuses for all of the things he didn't do. No video. No real phone records. No financial records. No DNA. No nothing. A real slop-job."

I asked, "Where do you think we should go from here?"

Taylor started, "I would say that Carbone is the only person in this part of the world with the wherewithal to buy off a police investigation. Somehow, my gut tells me that he is involved in one way or another. There are just too many coincidences with Tammy going missing before cameras were installed from a house given to her father, effectively, by Carbone. We really need to rule him in or out.

"To do this, we need to start with a look at the compound. I say the safest, if not the only, way to do this would be with a drone. If nothing else, we will be able to see how many guys they have and where they are concentrated."

"I agree," I responded.

I then moved to another subject, the proverbial elephant in the room. "How about last night?"

"What about it?" Taylor replied.

She then went on, "Oh, you mean our little tryst? Good for me. You?"

"I think you know how I feel. It's never been a secret."

She responded, "We can see each other from time to time. My main focus right now is Tammy. I think you know that. It doesn't mean that I don't have feelings for you. I do. And, frankly, I've grown to like you more as I see you away from your teaching gig. Let's just see how things go. It will work itself out."

"How about Frank? Do we keep him in the loop?"

"So, your passive-aggressive question really is do we still trust him enough knowing that he worked for a police force that we presume to be crooked?"

"Yes, that is my question."

"Well, balancing his usefulness with inside information against him turning on us, I have to go with the former. I vote to keep him involved. We could limit his involvement somewhat. I think he might know things about Carbone which he doesn't even know he knows."

She continued, "By the way, we cannot very well use the local police. Don't we suspect their involvement?"

"True. We will have to turn to the FBI. They have authority under the Hobbs Act to investigate local law enforcement. There is an office in Bryan. I'll make my calls, but I think we might do the drone thing first."

We were almost to her mom's house now. I dropped her off and asked, "Shall we meet with Frank tomorrow or should we look for a drone operator?"

"Both," she replied.

CHAPTER 26
The Drone Guy

I picked up Taylor at her mom's house at 10 a.m. Through a friend, who was neither in law enforcement nor lived anywhere near Newton or Haven, I got a referral for a drone guy willing to come to our location to meet us.

We were to meet him at my mom's house, which, as we know, is a farmhouse in rural Newton.

After picking up Taylor, she and I arrived at my mom's house at 10:20 a.m. Danny, the drone guy, was scheduled to arrive at 10:45. Frank was at work. We would meet with Frank in the evening at Smiley's.

Danny pulled up to my mom's in an older Toyota Camry.

"Hi guys. I'm Danny, the drone guy."

"I'm Rick, and this is Taylor. Nice to meet you."

"I understand that you are looking for some drone work."

"Yes. We want to photograph a large estate-type property located on top of a hill not too far from here."

Danny went on, "You know that since the passage of the FAA Modernization and Reform Act in 2012, there are many requirements for drone flight. I have a Part 107 certification from the FAA. Under the law, use by private citizens, such as you guys, is quite different than use by law enforcement.

"Under the law, private citizens need to stay lower than 400 feet, remain more than five miles from an airport, and use a relatively small drone, which I intend to do anyway.

"Civil Code Section 1708.8 is pretty clear. It provides that a person is liable for invasion of privacy when he knowingly enters onto the land or into the airspace above the land of another. In other words, if we get caught, you will definitely be at very least civilly liable to the property owner. In light of this, I will need an indemnity contract.

"Remember the 4th Amendment still applies. However, there is a distinction between examining inside of a house, where there is an expectation of privacy, and outside of the house, where there is a lesser expectation. We'll need to concentrate our efforts outside. The drone takes real-time video from which stills may be generated. I suggest being able to turn the video feed off and on in case we get near sensitive areas."

I asked, "Do you think that we can do this in such a way that the people on the ground won't know that we are looking at them?"

Danny replied, "I'll try, but they might hear the drone."

Danny and I agreed on a price and a time and a place to meet to look over the approach to the property. If the job was possible to do, we would make the final arrangements after looking at the site.

Danny left. I took Taylor back to her mom's place. As she got out of my car, she said that she had some things she needed to do for her mother and that we could meet at Smiley's at 7:30 with Frank.

"I'll see you and Frank at Smiley's tonight at 7:30 then."

She seemed fine with that.

CHAPTER 27

Letting Frank Go

We sat at our usual booth in the back.

Frank started, "How was the trip to see Detective Pratt? Did you get any information?"

I took up the response, "The trip was fine. The information we got was the information we already knew, no cameras, no real search, no DNA, no nothing. From that, I would say that we concluded that the investigative efforts were less than heroic.

"The trip was worth it in that we learned what we suspected. We learned that the job done by the police was so lackluster that the even police suspect that we suspect that they were involved. But it did not get us any closer to the resolution of Tammy's kidnapping."

Taylor added, "The guy was a real tool. If this is how he handled cases, I can't believe that he was a decorated detective, and I can't believe that you could work with him."

Frank replied, "I didn't work with him. I was getting coffee for the rest of the office in those days. He did, however, have a good reputation as a hard worker and diligent investigator. That's why this whole situation is so odd to me."

Taylor jumped in, "Too many coincidences for me. Tammy gets kidnapped just when her father may have had dealings with a gangster. He winds up with a big house and money. Historical coincidences are a little suspicious. Right, Rick? Isn't that what you told us in class?"

"I cannot argue with you there," I said. "The only connection we have left is between Fitzgerald and Carbone.

"When Taylor was visiting Bryan, she learned that that Carbone was using Fitzgerald as his front man to help with the Department of the Interior and Governor's Office in connection with his casino project. It appears as if Mr. Fitzgerald was taking a long time to deliver. Maybe Carbone got tired of waiting. Anybody who has put together an empire such as Carbone's is probably not only ruthless, but also impatient, wanting what he wants when he wants it."

I continued, "I think our next move is to surveil Carbone's compound with the drone to see if it makes sense to try to get a closer look on land.

"As we learned from Danny, there is some downside to this including civil liability, possible criminal liability, job loss, or worse. I would suggest that the two of you part ways with me now before things get out of control."

"No way," was Taylor's immediate response. "I got you into this mess, and I plan on seeing it through." Taylor then directed her comments to Frank, "Frank, though, should definitely sever his ties to us. You need to keep your job, and you cannot risk being connected with me, a known agitator and general pain. I know from our childhood days that being a policeman has always been very important to you, and I would hate to see you lose that."

"I agree," I said. "Frank should definitely drop out, and you should consider doing the same."

"Not on your life," was Taylor's response.

We broke up our little meeting. It was agreed that Frank would drop out and distance himself from the two of us. Taylor and I would carry on from here.

Before going any further, let me say that Frank had been invaluable to the enterprise. He was able to confirm what Taylor had heard on her trip to Bryan. He was able to confirm that there really is an Antony Carbone, that he really is a very bad guy, and that he really has a mountain-top compound. Frank was able to get the location of the compound without raising too much suspicion, a neat trick.

I arranged to meet with Danny at 5 a.m. the next morning near the road to Carbone's compound.

CHAPTER 28
Carbone's Compound

I picked up Taylor, and we drove well past Smiley's about an hour and a half north of Haven, pretty far from civilization. The road was one lane in each direction. A hillside extended up from the inside of the road. A canyon dropped off from the outside.

When one first enters the main road leading to the compound, he is traveling north. The road curves to the east. On the north side of the curve, a flat area opens up with an asphalt driveway leaving the main road at nearly a right angle. This driveway runs towards the ascending hill. At the base of the hill, there is a guardhouse which appears to be manned by one guard.

Past the guardhouse the private driveway begins its uphill ascent towards the main house. The private driveway continues a couple of miles up the hill to a motor court on the east side of the front door of the main house. From the pubic road, one may barely see the compound high on the hill.

There was one aspect of the topography that did seem to be in our favor. Because of the steepness of the hill, the driveway up to the house lists to the east. This makes the driveway approach to the east side of the house almost two miles long. If one wanted to reach the house by foot and was willing to hike, he would approach from the west, on the other side of the property from the driveway. The distance would be shorter, but the route would require hiking through steep, dangerous, and treacherous terrain.

Danny was pretty matter-of-fact. He said that the drone flight would not be difficult as there were no power lines or other aircraft in the area. We agreed on a price. I paid him. He agreed to do the drone work the next morning starting at around 7 a.m. He said that we could either be there or not. There would be a video of that which the drone observed, along with some stills. He said that he chose the time so that if he got caught, he could say that he was just doing some pleasure flying before work. If he chose an earlier time, that might be difficult to sell.

He thanked me for the check. Taylor and I returned to my car and drove back to Newton. On the way she asked me if I was planning on being present during the drone flight. I said that I was. She asked if she could come along. I said that I expected that she would.

We continued our drive to Newton. I thought I might gently bring up our relationship. She told me that she really liked being with me. We had a great time together which, for her, was more difficult to achieve than a quick romantic interlude. She said that she was attracted to me but that she was really overwhelmed with the work of tracking down Tammy's kidnapper. I said that I understood. What else could I say? Anything else might make it appear as if I only cared about her for romantic reasons.

CHAPTER 29

The Drone Flight

I picked up Taylor early in the morning to make it to the drone flight scheduled for 7 a.m. I mentioned to her that for the past several weeks, we had been looking for a connection between Tammy's kidnapping and someone capable of committing the crime. I was of the opinion that we had just about exhausted all of our possibilities.

Making a connection between the kidnapping and Carbone, or at least proving it, appeared to me to be quite a long shot.

I did mention that when my mother was alive, she had a local picker who would harvest her oranges every year. He said that the recent crops were of very poor quality. Apparently, there was an infestation of Asian Citrus Psyllid, a tiny winged insect that attacked various crops, including oranges.

I mentioned that I had spoken to two other farmers in the area who were experiencing the same thing. Was it a coincidence that just when Carbone needed land in Newton for a hotel and casino, a tiny winged insect would attack the crops growing on the very land he needed, reducing the value of that land?

Again, the coincidental theory of history was raising its head.

We met Danny at the road below the compound at 7 a.m. sharp. He told us that his plan was to fly the drone, take the video, and when the drone returned, download the video immediately to a flash drive. The flash drive would be hidden in the car. In this way, if the police or Carbone's men should apprehend us, we could just give them the drone. We would still have what we really needed, the flash drive.

The morning was perfect. Clear. No wind. The compound was only a little more than a mile from our location. Even when flying to the other side of the compound, the drone would not be more than 4 miles away and would remain virtually within our line of sight.

Danny launched the drone. It flew a couple of passes over the compound. It returned to us.

Danny quickly connected a USB cable and transferred the images from the drone to a flash drive. I took the flash drive, as I had paid for it.

Danny left in his car, and Taylor and I left in mine.

Taylor and I drove to the computer at my mom's house for a look.

We put the flash drive in the computer, and the drone's image came up on the screen. It was incredibly clear. From the drone footage, one could see the size of the compound. There were several buildings of different sizes and built for different uses. There was a large swimming pool and spa area with an adjacent building, probably a changing room. There was a large grass area adjacent to the largest structure, which appears to be the main house. There was a tennis court with its own changing rooms.

At the entry side of the house, the upper end of the driveway opened into a large motor court from which one would drop off visitors. The front door was adjacent to the motor court. Upon arriving at the compound, one would drop off his passengers at the front door, and the car would be driven either by him or by an attendant to an outdoor parking lot or to the garages.

On the opposite side of the house from the entry, there was a wing attached to the west side of the main house. Outside of this wing, there was a small grass yard with a swing set, sandlot, and other amenities generally used to entertain children. This yard was separately fenced and could only be accessed from the west wing.

In addition to the pool house, the tennis court house, the main house, and the smaller house, there were two additional structures, one perhaps for workers, and one which appeared to be a greenhouse. At the base of the driveway there was, of course, the guardhouse.

The entire improved portion of the property was encircled by a fence, probably electric.

Taylor focused in on the wing on the far west side of the main house and its separate yard.

She mused, "I never heard that Mr. Carbone had children or grandchildren. Why would he maintain a children's play yard at his compound? Who would use this area? Would he provide day care for his workers? From everything I've heard about him I would say that there is no chance that he would care enough about his employees for that. Also, from everything we have seen and heard, all of his employees are male, and all of them are want-to-be tough guys, which means no involved wives."

"I cannot disagree with your assessment," I replied.

Taylor continued, "Let's continue on with the drone footage and see what we can see."

It appears as if Danny made a first pass with the drone to give us an idea of the scope of the property, how many buildings were on the property, the relative location of the buildings, the position of the driveway approach and motor court, the position of the fence with respect to the buildings, and the location of the guardhouse. That portion of the video was approximately 30 minutes in length. Overall, the drone video was approximately 60 minutes in length. We had 30 minutes more to watch.

We watched the drone video for the remaining 30 minutes, and eagle eye Taylor noticed something that no mere mortal could see; ah, to have those young eyes.

A tiny speck could be seen exiting the west wing and entering the separate yard. Whoever this was spread out a large blanket on the grass, sat down in a low chair, and began to read a book, while, apparently, catching some sun.

Excitedly, Taylor exclaimed, "It's Tammy! I know it's Tammy! Carbone must have been holding her here!"

I did not share her certainty, though I thought it was possible. I must confess it was the only scenario that made any sense.

Here is where a little bit of knowledge can be less than helpful.

Taylor went on, "I've always heard that whatever a private citizen uncovers through an illegal search is still admissible in court and that the exclusionary rule is designed to apply to government agents and not to private citizens."

This left me to deliver the bad news, "This is true. However, even if the picture was enhanced, there would be no way that we could show that this image is Tammy, which would leave us no way to get a search warrant. The image is too small and grainy. If we went to the FBI with this, we would get laughed out of the office. Also, if we went to the authorities at all, Carbone would find out and move Tammy elsewhere, or worse.

"Further, while it is true that an illegal search by a private citizen might not be excluded as evidence, the person conducting the illegal search would still be civilly liable for trespass or some other tort and could be sued for money damages.

"We have to assume that Carbone has moles everywhere. If this is going to be done at all, we need to move quickly. We need to have enough evidence to get a warrant immediately, the first time, and to get agents to the house before Carbone can move Tammy."

Taylor replied, "Maybe I should hike up to the compound and see if I can get some better photos."

I was floored. All that I could think to say was this: "You must be out of your mind. You could get captured, killed, or worse."

Taylor said, "I don't see another way. I could try to get a job there, but I doubt that with everything going on he's hiring. I might be able to get in as part of the entertainment."

"All too risky," was all I could muster.

"But I have to do something. I'm going to hike in. Judging from the drone photos, I could move around the west side and up to the house. There is brush and other cover. I would then have to get past the fence to get close enough to take a photo."

"You know that the fence will probably be electric and that there are going to be roving guards all day and all night."

"I get all that, but there is no other option."

"I'm coming with you then."

"No way. You'll just slow me down, no offense."

"I can't let you go alone. If we do make it up there, remember to email each photo every time you take one. If you do get caught, the first thing they will do is take your phone."

Taylor asked, "Do you think I should arrange for some reinforcements?"

"Whom did you have in mind?"

"I thought I would ask my motorcycle club friends. I'm sure that when I tell Moose what I am doing he could arrange for himself and several friends to at least wait down by the main road as backup. He's a great guy, and his guys are pretty scary. I've helped him out with some stuff. In his mind, I think that he thinks that he owes me. This might be a good time to call in his marker."

I replied, "Since our initial look will be from a safe distance, perhaps we won't need him right now. We can always leave the compound and enlist his help if we think that we have something substantial."

Taylor said, "True."

Silly me. I took this to mean that Taylor agreed with me.

CHAPTER 29
At the Compound

Mr. Carbone summoned his chief of security to his private office. It was never a good thing to be summoned to your boss's office, regardless of what kind of business you're in.

When he arrived, Carbone asked, "Did you hear a buzzing above the compound early in the morning, around seven?"

"No."

"Who works graveyard?"

"Thompson."

"Call him and ask him. I don't know why I pay you guys. Such a waste of money."

"Sorry, sir. I will look into it and let you know."

"I certainly hope so."

CHAPTER 30

Taylor's Take on Herself

Taylor opined: Much has been said about me in this story. I have been described by some as equal parts beautiful, smart, and resourceful. By others, I have been described as a bitch on wheels. I consider myself to be a bitch when I need to be and a spoiled brat most of the time, even when I don't need to be.

As a young attractive woman on this planet, I have wide latitude. I can respond to you when it suits me and ignore you when it doesn't.

But all is forgiven because, face it, I am a young attractive woman on a planet where being young and attractive are probably the two most sought-after commodities.

What is the down side to all of these gifts you say? The downside is that I have to wonder if I will ever be taken seriously. A young man can get a degree, work in a field, and become respected, and when he states his opinion, be is taken seriously.

A young woman, on the other hand, may have all of the knowledge and experience of her male counterpart, but her opinions are dismissed. When she comes with her opinions, she is considered crazy or a conspiracy nut.

Am I jealous of this lack of parity? I must confess - a little.

To his credit, Rick is not a person who has ever been dismissive of me. He initially questioned my take on the events of Tammy's kidnapping. However, considering that all he knew of the events was what he learned from the internet, it makes sense that he would be skeptical.

I have to say that Frank too has always been supportive. To my knowledge, he has never discounted someone because of his or her race, religion, or gender, all to his great credit.

Of all of the guys out there, Rick and Frank are two of the good ones. I doubt that there are many, if any, who would put up with me and my extreme self.

It doesn't hurt that they are both good looking, but looks alone only keep things going in the very short run. Perhaps many young women would be willing to take a chance on a guy just because he is good looking, but I am not one of them. I've been through too much to take that kind of risk, but most women my age have not.

Frank has helped tremendously and gracefully bowed out. Rick has hung in with me in ways that baffle even me.

My thinking is that in life you can tell how someone feels about you not from what he says but by the way he treats you.

Rick treats me with the kind of respect and nurturing that I never dreamed possible. The kind of respect that I never thought I would have or deserve. If I could just let down some of my walls, I think we could have something really great. But I'm a basket case.

My mother never did anything but put me down. She never believed that I could accomplish anything or have anything to offer. She had a combination of the worst parts of the human condition. Part was jealousy. She was once attractive but is now a mess. She never developed any personal skills, and she could only survive by maintaining that no one else, particularly me, had any of those skills anyway.

My father ducked out early. He took the coward's way out and left me and my mother with very little. I used to wonder how he could do such a thing. But as I came to know my mother better, I could not blame him. I might have walked too.

Rick had two great parents who showered him with love, kindness, and opportunity. He's without excuses in the game of life. As for me, I hope it is not too late. It has often been said that too love someone else, you have to first love yourself. I hope that I can learn to love myself because I would really like to see how it feels to love someone.

I have plenty of room to cry foul. My father left us; I had to run the family business; my mother was an alcoholic, contributed almost nothing to our farm, and, on top of that was involved with some really bad guys, which could lap over onto me if I wasn't careful.

Rick and I are only part of the way through our journey, both with Tammy's case and with life. We have sent the drone. We learned a little, but not enough. What is left now is taking the hike up to the compound to see what we can see.

Let's see if we can weather this test together. Even with my mother and all of her baggage and me with all of my hang-ups, as crazy as it may sound, for reasons that I will never understand, I know that Rick loves me; I can only hope that I can evolve to a point where I can love him too. He's great, and he deserves it.

CHAPTER 31

The Meeting Before the Hike

I picked up Taylor very late at night, or early in the morning, about 3 a.m. We drove out to the Carbone compound, arriving about around 4:30.

When we arrived, we hid the car as well as we could along the side of the road and made our way back towards the clearing at the base of the driveway leading up to the compound. The compound could barely be seen at the top of the hill. There was much brush and steep terrain between the main road and the compound.

The driveway runs up the east side of the property. The motor court and the front door are on the east side. As a result, most of the vehicular and pedestrian traffic is on the east side.

This leaves the west side as the side less traveled which is good as the consensus of opinion is that Tammy is being held on the west side.

Taylor began. "We will need to hike towards the west side. The west side is furthest from the entry and other locations where guards are either stationed or roaming. It is further protected by another ascending hillside. My take is that it is too overgrown and treacherous to be considered a viable way to breach the compound. This would encourage the guards to patrol elsewhere."

After looking at the west approach, I thought to myself, 'and besides, no one in her right mind would be crazy enough to attempt to hike in by this route, except Taylor, of course.'

Taylor and I were both appropriately attired for the trip. Jeans, good hiking boots, long sleeve shirts, and small backpacks with water and a few essentials.

We started up the hill, making our way through the brush. It was over a one-mile hike. Oddly enough, there were some areas that looked as if they were part of a trail. This may have been a hiking area before the compound was built, or traversing the hill might have been necessary for the survey crews when the compound was being readied for construction.

Taylor and I encountered unpleasant loose soil, then rock, then overgrown brush cutting away at any exposed skin we might have, which was little. I had a machete to cut brush, so I was elected to lead the way.

We moved to the north; the terrain became even more steep and difficult.

As we moved towards the top of the hill, we came to the fence we saw on the drone footage. As suspected, it had a sign attached indicating that it was a high voltage electric fence. There would be no way that we could short it out or cut it without attracting the attention of the guards. Where the fence turned at a tree, there was a small opening along in its run. Taylor said that she could fit in but that I, at 6 feet, 170 pounds, could not.

She said, "I'll have to go it alone from here. You're never going to fit through that hole."

I replied, "No way. You can't go by yourself. Let's go back."

She said, "I have come too far to turn back now. There is no way I am going back. If you want to take me off of this mountain, you're going to have to kill me. So, give it up. I'm going in alone."

Things were beginning to spin out of control. I tried to reason with her. I said, "Let's call Moose and have him bring his team here before you enter the compound."

Taylor replied, "Okay, I'll call him."

Taylor took out her cellphone and called Moose. A woman answered the phone, "Hello, Motorcycle Enthusiasts of America."

"Hi, it's Taylor. Is this Carol?"

"Yes honey, what can I do for you."

"I need to speak with Moose. It's really important."

"Well, I'm sorry to say that he went camping with the boys."

Taylor asked, "Can you reach him. I wouldn't ask, but I really need to speak with him."

"You know as well as anyone else honey that cell phones are strictly prohibited on those camping trips. Back to nature and like that."

"When will he be back?"

"Tomorrow afternoon."

"Please have him call me at this number as soon as he comes in."

"I will."

I said, "I guess this means that we will hike down the hill and wait for Moose."

Taylor's reply, unfortunately, did not shock me. She said that she would hike up the hill and have a look and that I would hike down the hill to go for help.

She said, "You can drive to the camp site to find Moose. Just take the same road we came in on and get back onto the interstate. Turn north on I-7 and go to the Rock Ridge National Park turn off. At the end of the off-ramp, follow the signs to the park entrance. At the entrance, have the guard direct you to the rangers' office. They will know where Moose is camping. He's a regular."

I am sorry to report that things were left this way: She was hiking up the hill to try to breach the heavily armed compound of a known gangster, and I was hiking down the hill to try to round up help. I think they call that role reversal.

CHAPTER 32

Antony Carbone and Don Fitzgerald – The Connection

Let's just say that the Carbone family had being bad in its blood. Antony's grandfather came from Italy in 1915. He settled in New York. He had the good fortune to enter the crime business in the early 1920's, just about the time that the 18th Amendment made liquor illegal. The time was known as Prohibition.

During Prohibition, profits from bootlegging far exceeded profits which could be made from traditional crimes such as protection, extortion, gambling, and prostitution. Wars were waged over bootlegging, as it was a significant profit center.

Carbone's father took over the family business in the early 1940's, after Prohibition was repealed, and liquor became legal again. The vast money made from bootlegging allowed organized crime to expand into many other criminal activities, including loan sharking and drug trafficking.

As mid-century approached, organized crime infiltrated into the labor unions such as the Teamsters and the International Longshoremen's Association. This allowed crime families to make inroads into profitable legitimate businesses such as construction, demolition, waste management, and trucking.

Carbone's father moved the family to Las Vegas in the early 1960's, just after Antony was born in 1955. In the early 1960's, Castro took control of Cuba and shut down the gambling business. This caused gambling to move to Las Vegas. Perfect for the Carbone family.

As the third of three sons, it was unlikely that Antony would ever take over the very lucrative family business. He could see the handwriting on the wall.

As a testament to his "good fortune," a terrible "accident" took place. It has been reported that Antony's two older brothers were being driven together in one of the family limousines. The driver lost control, and the vehicle crashed through the highway barrier and cascaded down into a deep ravine, catching on fire. Everyone, including Carbone's two brothers, were killed instantly.

Through the years since the unfortunate "accident," it has often been rumored that Antony sabotaged the car's brakes. As I am told, no one had trouble believing the rumor, though you might not want to mention it to Antony unless you have a serious death wish.

Antony's father passed from a heart attack in 1985 when Antony was only 30. With his brothers gone, he was the only one left to take over the family business.

Antony was prolific. He was involved in sports betting, gas-tax fraud, labor racketeering, and drug smuggling through the several restaurants he owned. First Howard Hughes and then the RICO Act helped close down much of the organized crime in Las Vegas. Some gangsters turned states' evidence against others. By the 1970's, 1980's, and 1990's, most of the gangsters were leaving Las Vegas. Carbone stayed and kept his hand in it for a time. He did it all. Killing people, having people killed, running prostitutes, smuggling narcotics - a real choir boy.

In 2015, at 60, Carbone decided to opt out for the simple life. He moved to the California desert. There he could build a compound where he could live safely away from the organized crime figures he had so thoroughly infuriated. He had contacts with the local Police Commissioner and a couple of agents at the nearby FBI field office. Having bought them, he was free to do practically anything he wanted.

As we know, his plan was to do build a hotel and casino project at the south entrance to Rock Ridge National Park and to continue living at his compound. The project would be close enough to allow him to commute to work. He is old school. To Carbone, "no" is not an answer. If he wants something done, it gets done, or someone dies trying.

On a personal note, according to sources, Carbone is a person about whom a kind word has never been said. When he dies, he might be the first person in history for whom there will be no eulogy. They say that it is an even money bet whether six people can be collected to serve as pallbearers, and this will only occur if they can find six people who did not know him.

He is rich, wears expensive clothes, drives expensive cars, and has expensive jewelry, all of which he flaunts.

He is critical of everyone. He never supports a business associate or employee for any reason. He tears down everyone with whom he comes in contact.

When the subject of the "accident" comes up the consensus is that 'He killed his brothers, and he will kill many more along the way.'

He made a fortune of money, and he would not lose any of it.

As has been reported, his end game is a hotel and casino project in Newton at the south entrance to the National Park.

It is not enough that he has done all of the things attributed to him. He always needs an extra edge.

An absolutely necessary step towards building his casino project would be getting the interstate finished from Haven to Newton.

The people of Newton are small farmers of fairly simple means. They primarily grow oranges and sell them to brokers to sell elsewhere. Would Carbone pay the property owners of Newton the modest fair market value of their farms? Dream on; not Carbone.

It has been rumored that Carbone imported and let loose thousands of Asian Citrus Psyllid, a tiny winged insect that greatly damages orange crops.

These insects not only attack the leaves of the tree, but also make the fruit green and hard. They can be treated with a two-step insecticide approach, a direct spray followed by a soil-based treatment. However, many farmers will suffer greatly before they learn that their problem is related to an insect and how to exterminate them.

Carbone's long game has been to attack the crops so that he can pick up the farms at a discount. I call this comprehensively awful.

Don Fitzgerald was a high school football star. Not just a star, but a phenom. The best the State had ever seen. A quarterback who not only had a gun for an arm but who was fast, could break tackles, and had the moves of a running back. A real commodity in college and the pros.

He was such a standout at Haven High that he appeared as a man playing among boys. He was in his senior year. The plan was that he would finish at Haven High, get a scholarship to a top college, play for a time, and be tapped for a lucrative pro contract worth many millions of dollars over the years to come.

His girlfriend was, of course, the head cheerleader, Diane Williams. Don and Diane were crazy in love.

The team was off the weekend before their first post season game. Don and Diane, being so nuts about each other, decided to drive to Vegas and get married. After getting married, they returned to Don's small apartment which was rented for him by a team donor.

Don played in the first post-season game. Everything was going well, and it appeared as if the team would win easily and move on to the next round. However, late in the 4th quarter, Don was tackled hard, and some say illegally. As a result, he tore his ACL, and was carried from the field. The team won, but Don was injured.

The next day, Don was examined by a doctor who told him that he would never be able to play football again.

No scholarship, no pro contract, no prospects, and no skills on which to fall back.

Diane seemed okay with it all at first. She was still in love. She didn't really understand what not being able to play football would actually mean to their future.

The season ended. Don was able to finish school and graduate. He did not have the grades for a prestigious college, so he enrolled at Newton Junior College, the same school at which I am teaching now.

It was 1998. Don tried junior college for the next two years. He was not cut out to be a student. He did not like school, and he had no study habits. To his credit, he did take on a few odd jobs to try to make ends meet. Diane went to work as a waitress, which she hated. She had illusions of living the glamorous life as the wife of a pro athlete.

To complicate matters, Diane became pregnant. Their first child was born in 2001. He was a boy. They named him Jason.

With a wife and a child and no real job, Don became desperate. He decided to get his real estate license and go to work selling real estate. His thinking was that real estate was one of the few businesses where he might be able to make decent money without an advanced college degree.

He was well known and liked in the community. He was of the opinion that since he learned how to promote himself as an athlete, he could learn how to promote himself as a realtor, which he did.

Don did fairly well in the business over the next decade. In 2006, he and Diane had a second child, a daughter, Tammy.

After a decade in the business, Don felt he needed to figure out a way to make more money. He always felt that he let Diane down. He saw that the real money was not in commissions from sales but was from buying and selling. He had so many clients who bought properties and then re-sold them at a tremendous profit. He wanted to play in that game.

Because Don did not own anything himself and because his income was just enough to cover his expenses, he did not have the kind of credit necessary to buy and sell real estate in the way that he felt was necessary to generate profits.

Through his experience, however, Don figured out a way to use a straw buyer. A straw buyer is someone who buys something on behalf of another person. Don would have a straw buyer buy properties on his behalf, and he would then sell the properties at a profit.

This act is considered illegal if the transaction is consummated to commit fraud or if the person using the straw man cannot legally make the purchase on his own due to his poor credit.

If a person with good credit secures a loan and buys a home for a person with poor credit with no intention of living in the home or making the mortgage payments, the act of securing the loan constitutes mortgage fraud which is a criminal offense.

Over the next several years, Don was doing very well buying and selling properties using the straw man approach. To purchase more valuable properties, he figured out a way to borrow the down payment so he would not have any of his own money in the deal. This is also illegal.

Before embarking on this venture in earnest, Don opened his own business. Everything was going well until he received a call from Police Commissioner John Burrows. Commissioner Burrows knew Don from his football days. He could see that Don was doing a little too well in real estate and began making inquiries. He coerced someone to rat out Don. This allowed Burrows to learn about Don's illegal dealings.

Burrows offered Don two options. He could either be arrested for fraud or he could become available to "help out" as needed. Don opted for the later.

Don heard nothing more from the Commissioner for the next several months.

As to Carbone, as we know, he moved to the desert in 2015 to work on his casino project.

As we know, presently, there were two main entrances to Rockridge National Park, a north entrance and a south entrance. From Haven, the north entrance is quite far. The south entrance, on the other hand, was much closer. However, before the extension of the interstate, reaching the south entrance was not only difficult but was actually dangerous as it required one to drive over a dangerous mountain pass road.

In short, the road was so dangerous that the vast majority of tourists and campers opted to drive all of the way to the north entrance rather than risk the drive over the mountain road to the south entrance. This resulted in the south entrance being rarely used.

Carbone learned that to encourage tourists to use the south entrance, it would be imperative to greatly improve the road from Haven to Newton.

For 2015 and most of 2016, Carbone made several attempts on his own to persuade the Planning Commission and the City Council to extend the interstate highway through Haven to Newton.

His attempts were rebuffed. He was told that to construct such a significant road, it would be necessary to show a community need. It was reasoned that it was not enough to show that a business person needed a road for his own pet project; others would also have to benefit. Also, Carbone's reputation apparently preceded him. A known dangerous gangster is bound to be turned down for a municipal project.

Desperate, Carbone called Burrows.

"John, these locals are killing me. I asked them to extend the interstate highway from Haven to Newton, and they turned me down cold. They said that I would need to show that the new highway was necessary for a community need. Imagine that."

Burrows replied, "Maybe you should get a lawyer and see if there is some legal loophole which could be used to build your highway."

Carbone countered, "John, that is really too much trouble and probably will not work. What I really need is my own, personal local front man. I need someone well known in the community. This person will have to be smart enough to come up with something resembling a community need for the new road but who is not bright enough to understand exactly why it is needed, at least during the beginning stages. Also, it would help if this person is a little dishonest.

"If the Planning Commission or the City Council found out that I was planning a casino, the project would never be accepted. In other words, honesty could blow my entire project."

Commissioner Burrows responded, "So you need someone smart enough to get a significant roadway approved but dumb enough to not really grasp what he is doing? It would also help if he was at least a little dishonest."

"Yes."

Burrows blurted out, "I have the perfect guy for you. His name is Don Fitzgerald. He's well known in the community after 15 years in the real estate business, but he is dumb as a rock and a little dishonest. I have a criminal investigation hanging over his head right now.

Carbone replied, "He sounds perfect. When do I get to meet this moron?"

"I can arrange it for as soon as tomorrow."

"Good. We can meet at the compound at 12."

"Okay."

The next day came, and Burrows and Don met with Carbone at his compound.

After introductions, Carbone started, "Did John tell you what I need?"

Don answered, "Yes. He said that you need to extend the interstate from Haven to Newton but that the City Council and the Planning Commission turned you down. He said that you were told that you would need to show a community purpose for the work to even be considered."

Carbone replied, "That is correct."

Don said, "I understand. The locals are pretty protective of their own. You might consider doing this. You might consider proposing a residential subdivision in the pass between Haven and Newton. They would then have to extend the interstate because otherwise there would be no way to reach the place safely. You need to emphasize safety. Obviously, the subdivision could be reached, but it could only be reached over the existing dangerous mountain road.

John interjected, "Do you think that would work?"

Don continued, "Yes. They have been dying for someone to build luxury housing close to Haven for years, but no one saw any money in it."

Carbone asked, "Could you do such a project?"

Don replied, "Yes. I have been approached by several people who own tracts of land in the pass who would love to sell. Remember, raw land is a tricky thing. Someone has to spend some real money to buy raw land and then hope that it winds up in the path of development.

"The owner, while waiting for development to reach his land, has to pay taxes, clear brush, insure, fence, maintain, and hope that someone doesn't fall down hiking and sue. More often than not, it is the children or grandchildren of the forward thinkers who ultimately cash in.

"I have a couple of 70 or 80-acre tracts that have been touted to me in the past couple of years."

Carbone, ever the impatient one, asked, "How long will it take to get the project going?"

"It is a fairly long process. Land in California cannot be divided for sale unless the developer complies with the Subdivision Map Act. The developer selects a team including a surveyor and engineer. The team meets with the Planning Commission, Zoning Administrator, and Building Department to discuss feasibility, including whether utilities, drainage, sufficient roads, sufficient lots, and areas for open space, parks, schools, and animal sanctuaries can be achieved.

"Provided that there are more than five parcels proposed, a Tentative Map would be drawn up. Once the Tentative Map is drawn up, the matter is often set for public hearing before the City Council or Planning Commission. If approved, a Final Map is filed. The County Recorder uses the term Tract Map instead of Final Map setting out the lots.

"This all takes time."

Carbone, crass as usual, asked Don, "What do you want from all of this?"

Don thought and then replied, "I want the largest house in the subdivision and the exclusive right to sell the remaining lots or houses, for which I will get the commissions."

Carbone replied, "I guess that if this is what it is going to take to get the interstate through I will have to do it. I won't be able to execute the rest of my plan without that road."

"What is the rest of your plan?" Don asked.

"To build a hotel and casino in Newton near the south entrance to Rock Ridge National Park. You realize that I expect you get that through too."

"I don't know if I can do that. I don't know anything about the casino business."

"Well, I expect you to learn."

Burrows and Carbone had really worked Don into a corner. This deal was the only way Don was ever going to get the big house and steady income he felt he deserved. He was afraid that if he turned Carbone down flat, he would never have a chance at either one again, and could even go to jail, if Burrows wished.

So, stupidly, as to the casino part of the project, he did not say that he could not do it. He just left it ambiguous, figuring he could re-negotiate after the subdivision was completed. Carbone, of course, chose to hear what he wanted to hear, which was that Don would undertake the entire project, including the casino portion.

It was 2016, and from this, the uneasy partnership between Don Fitzgerald and Antony Carbone was born.

Before going ahead, it should be emphasized that each of one of them disliked the other intensely. Carbone felt that Don was a pampered mama's boy who never worked a day in his life, which was mostly true.

Don felt that Carbone was a mean and nasty criminal who would step on anyone or anything to get his way, which was actually true.

Don lit into the subdivision and interstate extension part of the project with a vengeance. He worked night and day and made incredible headway.

The project was 70 acres. Around the front, there were 1,500 square foot townhomes looking onto the main public road. Behind the townhomes, there were 2,500 square foot single family homes with Spanish style stucco exteriors and tile roofs.

To enter the subdivision, one passed through a first gate. This gate allowed access to the several cul-de-sacs lined by the townhomes and homes. Inside of the project towards the rear, there was a second gate. This gate provided access to the large lots with the large homes in the rear. The large homes ranged in size from 5,000 to 6,000 square feet and included the 8,000 square foot mansion that was built for Don. A fire road extended from the back of the project to a seldom used access road.

By the middle of 2018, the interstate extension was complete, some of the homes were nearly finished, and other of the homes were in various stages of construction.

By pressing hard, Don was able to have his personal residence, though not finished, finished enough for the family to move in.

Don, Diane, Jason, and Tammy moved into their new 8,000 square foot mansion in October of 2018.

When the Fitzgerald family moved in, the subdivision was clearly not finished. The guard houses were barely up and were not manned, there were no video cameras, and the guard patrols were, at best, sporadic. But they were so anxious to change their life style that they moved in anyway.

Don was never happier. He felt that he was finally delivering on his promise of a great life to Diane and his family

Diane was ecstatic. She felt vindicated for the years of hard work at menial jobs while raising two children. This was going to be a new life-style for her.

The relationship between Don and Carbone, however, did not improve. In fact, it began to further deteriorate. Carbone felt that Don was concentrating all of his efforts on Don's part of the project, that is, the interstate and his own house, while neglecting Carbone's part, the hotel and casino.

Carbone called Burrows and complained bitterly about Don and his ineptitude with respect to the casino. He wanted Burrows to order Don to come to the compound for a chat. Burrows arranged for Don to meet Carbone at the compound for, we presume, his dressing down.

Don drove to the compound, checked in with the guard, and was directed, as were all visitors, to the motor court. An attendant took his car and parked it in the adjacent lot. Don was met by a guard at the front door and shown into Carbone's private office.

Carbone's private office was really quite spectacular with wood paneling, book shelves from floor to ceiling, leather chairs, a beautiful oil painting over the fireplace, and numerous reproductions and art objects scattered around the room.

After exchanging pleasantries Carbone started, "Well Don, I am really disappointed with you. You've spent over a year working on your part of the project while neglecting my part."

Rather than just apologizing for what was actually the truth, Don became defensive. He tried to reason with Carbone, something which was often tried but was never successful.

Don retorted, "That's not really true. I got the interstate completed. You would need to get that done to have a casino under any circumstances. I tried to tell you that I had no experience with casinos when we first met, but you wanted me to go ahead anyway."

Don, nervously, continued, "We are going to need to get a specialist on board. I've talked to a couple of people. I've been told that only Indian tribes can have casinos in California and that those casinos can only be built on Indian Reservations."

What Don was telling Carbone was not entirely true. While it is true that only Indian tribes can have casinos and while it is also true that it is far easier to build an Indian casino on an Indian Reservation, it is possible to build an Indian casino on property other than an Indian Reservations under certain circumstances.

The federal Indian Gaming Regulatory Act permits gaming on lands which are not technically part of an Indian Reservation. This would include lands taken into trust for the benefit of an Indian tribe if the Secretary of the Interior determines that it would be in the best interest of the tribe and would not be detrimental to the surrounding community. Further, the Governor would have to concurs with the determination.

Don tried to explain all of this to Carbone.

Instead of trying to understand, Carbone became enraged, typical conduct for a spoiled and entitled thug. Carbone lit into Don saying, "Don, it's your job to get the casino built. I don't care if you need to bribe every Indian in the State. Just get it done."

Don replied, "I just don't have the pull to do that part of the job. Can't you get someone else? I don't even know how to approach an Indian tribe, the Secretary of the Interior, or the Governor."

Carbone continued his rant, "Have you secured a site for the casino. It will take at least five acres."

"I have made inquiries. I can get the five acres. It will cost us a little more than we thought. The local farmers figured out the pest infestation that they were experiencing and have hired an exterminator to deal with it. Apparently, they were successful. Now they feel that their farms are worth fair market value; something we did not figure.

Don continued, "I held off securing the land because I needed to first find out if we could get permission to build a casino on it. I didn't want you to own five acres in the middle of nowhere if we couldn't build the casino. Otherwise, you would be stuck with a luxury hotel for a few campers going into the park. It would be a huge money loser."

Carbone, now livid, told Don, "You have put me in a position where I am going to have to light a fire under your feet to get you moving. You have fritted away nearly two years with this. I feel that you have duped me. You pursued and completed your part of the project, and I have heard that you recently moved into your new mansion. But you barely started my part. You played me. You got what you wanted, and now you are looking to get fired so the project can be passed off to someone else to finish. This is a dangerous game you are playing."

Don replied, "I will try to see what I can do with the casino part of the project."

Carbone said only, "You do that."

The Fitzgerald family was allowed to live in their new house for just two more days when the unspeakable happened:

Their young daughter, Tammy, was kidnapped from her bedroom.

The Haven-Newton Police Department was called in. The den, which was connected through a double wide door opening to the living room, was converted into a command center. Phone extensions were attached to the house land line.

Diane was beside herself with grief. Crying non-stop for hours on end. She could not sleep. She could not eat. To add to her grief, she felt guilty. With her new found financial and social position, she was highly sought after for charities and other civic activities. She felt that because of her charitable and civic activities, she might not have paid enough attention to her young daughter.

Taylor was with Diane trying to be helpful in any way possible.

No ransom demand came.

The police investigation started. Phone records were checked. There was only one incoming or outgoing call, an incoming call to Don from his regular gardener.

DNA samples were taken. A search, of sorts, was made of the grounds around the house and subdivision.

The investigation seemed somewhat low-key. Don seemed distracted. He did not push the police as hard as one might expect. One would presume that he knew that it was Carbone who kidnapped Tammy to encourage him to work harder on the casino project.

2018 was drawing to a close. The family decided that it wanted a funeral before the end of the year. The funeral took place on December 28, 2018, during the week between Christmas and New Year's.

Presuming that Carbone's plan was to kidnap Tammy to encourage Don to work harder on the casino project, it was a poor plan at best, as were most of Carbone's plans.

Don, who was busy all of the time finishing the subdivision and moving into his new home, was placed on double duty as he had to remain around the house to help with the investigation and answer the phone if a ransom call came in. This greatly cut into his time for the casino project, the very thing Carbone wished to avoid. Apparently, Carbone was not known for being smart, and it was showing.

Don reached out to a few Indian tribes, but everyone knew he didn't know what he was doing. After New Year's, as things started up again, he recommitted to finding a willing tribe and continuing in his quest to partner with it for a casino.

A couple of months later in early 2019, Taylor decided that she would start up an investigation of her own, a sort of parallel investigation. She began asking questions and doing what she could. She was viewed as a nuisance by the police. This makes sense as they were both inept and complicit, a bad combination for successful police work.

Detective Pratt retired and moved to Mount Shasta.

In March, Don hired an attorney who specialized in Indian casinos. He told Don that he would look into the matter. He and Don met again in April, 2019.

He told Don that the case of United Auburn Indian Community, etc. vs Brown was up on appeal. He said that in that case, a tribe applied for permission to build a casino on Indian lands taken into trust for the tribe. In other words, they were seeking permission to build a casino on land which was not technically on an Indian Reservation, similar to Don's case.

He told Don that the Governor approved the project, and it appeared as if construction would be moving forward.

However, a competing tribe sued to stop the project contending that the permission that the tribe needed had to come from the legislature and could not come from the Governor alone.

It was still 2019. Under the law as it existed in 2019, it was uncertain whose permission would be necessary, the Governor or the legislature.

Ultimately, in 2020, the Supreme Court of California held that the Governor alone could grant permission for an off-Reservation casino project. However, this was not the law in 2019. In 2019, the United Auburn case was still up on appeal making it uncertain whose permission was necessary, further complicating Don's mission.

Throughout 2019, Don continued to work to either find someone to help him or to get the project through himself, but he was unable to do so.

Throughout the Spring and Summer of 2019, Taylor continued her investigation which was not successful. She had just about given up when she enrolled in my class in September, 2019. When she learned that I worked in the DA's office and had some investigative experience, her interest in Tammy's case was renewed.

She thought that she found people with whom she could work. For her renewed investigation, she enlisted me and Officer Frank Diaz.

Our investigation into Tammy's kidnapping put us on a collision course with Antony Carbone and Don Fitzgerald. In 2019, these were the events as they unfolded.

Don spent most of the year trying to find an Indian tribe with which to partner for the casino project.

Taylor, Frank, and I conducted our investigation.

Carbone went on with business as usual, including holding Tammy prisoner at his compound.

We return now to the events leading up to the show down between Taylor and Carbone.

Please trust me when I say that I was just an observer in this affair. It was Taylor's strength of character, along with the help of Moose and his people, that brought things to their ultimate conclusion.

CHAPTER 33

The Rest of My Hike and Day

As we remember, Taylor and I parted ways on the hill adjacent to Carbone's compound. She was going to breach the fence for a closer look, and I was going to find Moose at his camp site to ask for his help.

Though unpleasant, the hike down the hill was easier than the hike up. I reached the car with only a few minor scratches from the brush and a little dirt. It was now morning.

As you recall, Taylor and I hiked up to the west side of the improved part of the property to see if there was any evidence that Tammy was being held there.

When we reached the electric fence, it was decided that because of my size, I could not get through the one small opening in the fence. Against my repeated protests, Taylor decided to stay and try to get a closer look. Unable to reach Moose by phone, I was directed to go to the Rock Ridge National Park where Moose was camping to try to persuade him to come to the compound to help Taylor.

As instructed, I started the car and headed towards the camp grounds to find Moose. When I arrived at the entrance, I was directed to the ranger station. I knocked on the door and was let in. I asked if they knew Moose. They said that they did. I said that I needed to contact him and that it was an emergency.

I was instructed to park my car in the lot. I would then have to hike to the camp grounds near the north ridge. I would probably be able to find Moose or at least someone from his party.

I parked, hiked, and arrived at the camp grounds. I encountered someone who looked as if he could be a military service veteran. I asked him if he knew Moose.

His reply was, "Who wants to know?"

"I'm a friend of Taylor's, and she needs me to get a message to Moose."

"I know her. If you know her, you must be okay. Moose is upstream fishing. Just follow that trail. You can't miss him."

I hiked up the trail along the river. A gentleman matching Moose's description was fishing along the river bank. I asked, "Are you Moose?"

"Yes." He replied.

"Is it okay to call you Moose?"

"My real name is Giovanni Moustaka, if that works better for you."

"No. Thanks. Let's go with Moose."

"What's up?" He asked.

"It's about Taylor. I think you know her. She's gotten herself into a bit of trouble."

"What kind of trouble?"

"I presume you already know about the kidnapping of the 12-year-old girl she was babysitting. Taylor was having trouble wrapping her head around the whole thing and undertook her own investigation of the crime."

Moose said, "I heard that the little girl's father was helping Antony Carbone, the gangster, bring the interstate through to Newton."

"Yes. Unfortunately, however, that was only the first step of his plan. His end game was to have the new interstate make the land around the south entrance to Rock Ridge National Park, this park, more suitable for his hotel and casino project.

"As ridiculous as it might sound, Carbone actually expected Mr. Fitzgerald to persuade the Department of the Interior and an Indian tribe to allow the casino to be built on property which is not part of an Indian Reservation.

"Do you think it would be beneath Carbone to kidnap Mr. Fitzgerald's daughter to persuade him to finish his job?"

Moose's reply was short, to the point, and with no frills: "No."

Moose then asked, "Where is Taylor now?"

I then, sheepishly, told him my sad tale, "We sent a drone over Carbone's compound and saw an area where Carbone could, if he wished, keep a child captive. However, what we saw would not be enough to get a warrant. Taylor decided to hike up the hill to see if she could get a closer look.

"We reached an electric fence. We found an opening in the fence just large enough for her, but not large enough for me. So, we agreed that she would carefully look around and that I would return to find you in case anything went wrong."

Moose exploded in a way that I had never seen before and hope to never see again. He lit into me screaming, "If anything went wrong? What could possibly go right? You left a 19-year-old girl on the side of a mountain to sneak into the compound of one of the most dangerous criminals in the world by herself, unarmed?

"You are either an idiot, which I am beginning to think is probably the case, or you don't care whether she lives or dies, because she will probably be dead very soon, if she's not dead already. I sincerely hope that you are kidding me with this story. No one, not even you, could be that stupid."

I replied, "Sorry. That is the true story."

Moose continued, "I am only doing this because it's Taylor, and I know that her heart is in the right place. I understand that she can't live with the prospect of the little girl being held captive by these creeps. But, she should have come to me first. Now I will have to undo the damage already done before I can fix it.

"I am going to have to call in 20 years of favors to raise enough people to get her out of there, if that is even possible at this point.

"I will have to leave camp now to return home to get started contacting my people. The five guys with me her are in for sure. I don't even have to ask. When I leave, they will break camp and meet me and anyone else I can enlist at Smiley's later. I'm going to need at least 12 guys, including me."

I said, "I'm going to try with the FBI."

"If you must, please do it at a time when it is too late for them to contact the local police. If the police find out, they will call Carbone which might cause him to kill both of the girls, on the spot."

I replied, "I really have no choice but to call."

Being sufficiently brow-beaten, I returned home to wait to hear from Moose about whether he was able to raise enough people to assault the compound, and, if so, when and where they would assemble.

As much as Moose dislikes me, he still needs me as I am the only person with first-hand knowledge of where me and Taylor entered the property and reached the fence.

Moose left to raise his people. I went home to wait for his call and to call the FBI. The rest of Taylor's day is coming up.

CHAPTER 34

The Rest of Taylor's Hike and Day

I am really a wimp. I suffered a few cuts and bruises and some dirt on my clothes getting down the hill and to the car. To add insult to injury, I was then severely dressed down by Moose when he found out that I left Taylor on the hillside outside of the compound. This probably would have bothered me more except for the fact that I had to agree with him.

Days later I learned how the rest of Taylor's day went. Yikes. It made my day look like a vacation in Hawaii.

Taylor was able to get through the hole in the electric fence. She was able to work her way to the back of the house and the private yard. She was able to get as far as the separate fence for the private yard. Tammy had come out of the house and into the private yard. It was after noon now. She was too far away and engrossed in her daily routine to notice Taylor.

Taylor recognized her as Tammy. Even though she was several months older, she looked very similar to how Taylor remembered her. Unfortunately, though, there was a sadness in her little eyes; the eyes that used to sparkle with joy when Taylor would come over to babysit were now cloudy and muted.

Tammy's mother was a nice lady, but since her husband had come into money, she had become so engrossed in charities and society functions that she didn't have much time for the children. The boy was already old enough so it didn't matter. Tammy, on the other hand, was just reaching the age when she needed guidance from her mother.

Though her mother loved her, she was not getting everything she needed from her. This caused her to latch onto Taylor, who really did her best to be a good role model.

Taylor and Tammy developed a closeness that is unusual. The kind of closeness that is most often reserved only for family.

Taylor instructed her about make-up, clothes, shoes, and, most importantly, boys. At 12, Tammy was just starting to notice the opposite sex. Taylor, because of her looks, was hit over the head with it, even before she was Tammy's age. Taylor was hoping that she could help Tammy get past some of the mistakes she made. Maybe wishful thinking.

Taylor motioned to try to get Tammy's attention. It finally worked. Tammy noticed her. Taylor motioned for her to come closer. Tammy moved towards her carefully, as if she did not know that the person summoning her was someone she knew. Finally, as Tammy got closer, she recognized the person as Taylor.

She ran to Taylor and tried to touch her through the fence of her private yard. "You came for me. You remembered me. All of these months, I thought that you and my family forgot about me and were going to leave me in this horrible place with these awful people."

Taylor, heartbroken, but not wishing to show it, said, "I have never given up on finding you. I have done everything. But I was powerless. Everyone thought I was a crackpot. I finally met a nice man, one of my teachers, who has been a great help, and he has also worked very hard to find you."

Reality then set in when Tammy asked, "What are we going to do now? These people are never going to let me go, and if you get caught they might do bad things to you."

Taylor said, "Maybe I should try to get out of here and get some help."

Just then, the first security guard, a large goon-like man in a dark suit, grabbed Taylor from behind. Remembering her hand-to-hand combat lesson from Bart, she grabbed his arm, twisted it, and drove him to the ground. Once on the ground, she began kicking him in the neck, face, groin, and everywhere else she could. As she remembered, her legs were much stronger than her arms, which proved to be the case.

The first guard was temporarily out of commission when a second guard came at her face-to-face. She was able to get her hands up, open fist, as she had been instructed. The second guard came at her with a right, as she expected. She was able to deflect his arm to the left and give him a backhand move to his neck.

Temporarily immobilized, she fish hooked his nose and eyes, causing him to cry out in pain. She then smashed his nose with an open fist, driving him to the ground next to the first guard. She used her legs to beat him best she could.

A third guard was inside of the house and heard the commotion. He grabbed a stun gun and exited to the fight location. He was able to get the stun gun to Taylor's neck, which put her on the ground and out of commission for long enough for the three guards to restrain her and take her inside.

She was taken to a room in the house. She would later find out that this room was known as the "security" room. She was strapped into a metal chair bolted to the concrete floor. The chair was about three feet from the wall.

After she was secured, the guard with the stun gun said, "What were you doing snooping around the compound?"

"I was hiking and got lost." She replied.

Taylor didn't think that this explanation would work, but it was the best she could come up with on the spur of the moment. The other two guards, who were pretty badly beaten, left to get cleaned up.

The third guard remained and continued with his line of questioning, "You were just hiking, by yourself, on private property, on a hillside with no trails, in an area posted 'do not trespass', and got lost after making contact with someone living on the property?"

"Yes."

"Do you know the person you saw?"

"No. Never seen her before."

He left, leaving Taylor strapped to the chair.

A few minutes later, the security guards returned with an older, Italian-looking gentleman. He looked distinguished, wearing a $5,000 suit and very expensive shoes. He had a Patek Philippe watch. His grey hair was coiffed, and he was gently tanned. He was definitely not one of the hired help.

The third security guard started, "Mr. Carbone, we found this young lady snooping around the compound and talking to the little girl in the private yard."

Carbone said, "Is that so? Well, young lady, do you know this girl?"

Taylor replied, "No. Never seen her before."

Carbone went on, "You were just out for a hike in a restricted area, breached an electric fence, saw a young girl, and began talking to her?"

"Yes."

"And when confronted by a first security and then a second security guard, you engaged in a fight with each of them?"

"No. They engaged in a fight with me. I would have been perfectly willing to leave and hike back down the hill, if they would have allowed me to."

"Pardon me if I tell you that I don't believe you. Allow me to ask you again, do you know the girl?"

At this point, Taylor was in pretty bad shape. Though she got the better of the two guards, they did inflict some injuries. She looked pretty beaten up. In an effort to remain cool and unwilling to give in, she calmly replied, "No."

Carbone was addressing the three security guards, "Go, get the little girl, and bring her here. We'll see who knows what."

He continued, "You must think we are really stupid. All you are going to accomplish is getting a beating for the girl."

A few minutes later the three guards and Tammy returned to the room. The four looked on as Carbone addressed Taylor, "I am going to ask you one more time, why are you here, and what do you know, or think you know? If you do not tell me right now, we are going to first beat the girl and then start on you. Eventually, you will tell us. You might as well save the girl and yourself a beating."

"Okay. Okay. But please take the girl back to her room. Then I will tell you what you want to know."

Carbone motioned to the three security guards, and they took Tammy out of the room and back to another room in the house.

"Now, tell me now what you are doing here."

At this point, it did not look as if she and Tammy had a chance of making it out alive so she figured she might as well try at least part of the truth. If Carbone heard at least some of the things she knew, he might become mad enough to do something stupid, which might make him vulnerable.

Taylor started, "To tell you the truth, I was Tammy's babysitter. After Tammy disappeared, I never believed that she was really dead, so I started my own investigation. I interviewed the lead detective. Either he was painfully stupid or somehow complicit in her disappearance. I think both. The fake search. No body found. No ransom. The poor collection of physical evidence. No phone records. No financial records.

"I heard that Mr. Fitzgerald helped with the permits to build Haven Lakes and to complete the interstate from Haven to Newton. I heard that this was not all you wanted from him. I heard that you also wanted him to get the Department of the Interior and an Indian tribe to allow you to build a casino at the south entrance to Rock Ridge National Park, far from an actual Indian Reservation.

"No offense, but anyone with half a brain would know that this was far beyond Mr. Fitzgerald's capabilities.

"Then if that wasn't enough, to pressure Mr. Fitzgerald to do that which he was not equipped to do anyway, you kidnapped his daughter.

"Apparently, your plan was to hold his daughter until he could come through with permission to locate a casino away from an Indian Reservation. Silly plan. Again, no offense."

This exchange made Carbone nothing short of apoplectic. He became completely unhinged and screamed, "I'll tell you what is silly. You coming up here and getting caught. Now I have two people to get rid of."

Taylor tried her trump card, "That may be difficult. You see by now everybody knows we are here. It's just a matter of time before they come up here after us. Kidnapping and killing two unarmed girls will certainly not sit well with anyone, and you could wind up in the electric chair, or worse, in prison in the general population where you will become somebody's wife, until you're shanked. Inmates countenance many things, but killing unarmed children is not one of them."

Carbone became so enraged that he went completely off the rails. If nothing else, Taylor really knew how to push his buttons.

In an effort to be as dismissive as possible, Carbone said, "Well, little missy, we will see about that. I own all of the law enforcement around here. That idiot detective took money that can easily be traced to him. The Commissioner, who barely has a functioning brain, is even more bought and paid for. He's been mine for years. We can kill you and the girl, and no one will do a thing."

"Well, then, I hope you also own the FBI. The Federal Kidnapping Act authorizes the FBI to investigate kidnappings."

Carbone was now really agitated, "They won't do anything. I own them, too."

Taylor decided to throw everything she had at him. She said, "I think that you would be better off letting us go. If you let us go and the public does not find out, law enforcement will be able to sweep what has happed so far under the rug. Neither of us has been too badly hurt. If you kill us and the public finds out, the public outcry will be so great that law enforcement will be unable to protect you, even if you do own them.

"The other thing you don't know is that you may own the local yokels at the Haven-Newton Police Department and even at the local FBI field office, but I have something you don't have. I have friends. And most of my friends are ex-Seals and Rangers.

"Please believe me when I tell you that they are a scary bunch, and the last thing that they like is a prissy a-hole like you who preys on women and children. When they are done with you, you will be in such a world of hurt that you will be begging them to finish you off to put you out of your misery."

At this, Carbone lost it, "Why don't you keep you trap shut. You think you are so smart, but you're the one tied up here. Now I need you to tell me, who else knows about this?"

"Why? You claim that you own everyone anyway. What difference does it make who knows?"

Carbone replied, "It will make it easier for me to cover my tracks if I know who knows. So, I ask you again, who knows?"

"Screw you."

Carbone then reared back and slapped Taylor across the face.

A little shaken but remaining outwardly serene Taylor replied: "And here I thought chivalry was dead."

Carbone said, "I'm going to make an example out of you. Sneaking onto my property. So I ask you again who knows about his?"

Taylor replied: "F-you."

Now looking for ways to buy time, Taylor went on, "Let me fight one of these a-holes."

Carbone replied, "Oh, that would be too easy. Any of my security guards would love to take a crack at you."

"Two of them already got their asses kicked by me. If it wasn't for that chicken-shit stun gun, I would be long gone by now."

It was early evening. Taylor's banter must be credited for keeping her alive for several hours. Carbone still thought he needed the information that Taylor had and was running out of patience. Fuming, he said to his guards, "Go get the waterboarding stuff."

Waterboarding was his torture of choice. Any other form could either leave scars or marks which would be difficult to deny.

Carbone re-entered the security room, "We are going to get you ready for waterboarding now. You might reconsider telling me what I need to know."

"Screw you," was Taylor's response.

Taylor had some experience with waterboarding from her lessons with the Doctor of Pain on her camping trip with Moose and his friends. She just needed to get past the initial rush of water.

Carbone's guys tied Taylor to a board. They tilted the board back so her face would be on a backwards slant. A cloth was put over her face, and water was poured over the cloth. She could feel water entering her mouth and nose, reaching her sinuses.

She knew that if she could handle the water in her sinuses, she would be alright. After receiving the first dose of water, she was okay, but pretended to be drowning. Not wanting to kill her, the guards tilted her upright. The water left her sinuses.

"Do you want more, bitch, or do you want to tell me who knows about you and your little mission?"

Taylor made no reply.

"Again, who knows about this?"

There was no reply from Taylor.

Carbone continued, "Let's try this again."

They waterboarded her a second time, then a third time, and then a fourth time. It was getting late, and Carbone and his guys were getting tired. They actually looked worse than Taylor.

"Okay, guys, let's get back to this first thing tomorrow morning. We will be fresh and can really have some fun with this bitch."

Taylor was untied from the board and was taken to a room in the west wing where she would remain with one of the security guards until morning when, she was told, her waterboarding would resume.

It appears as if she was able to keep the two of them alive, at least until morning. She hoped that this would be enough time for Moose to raise his people and get to the compound.

CHAPTER 35

Back to Moose

As we see, my day was a little rough, but Taylor's was downright horrible. She was engaged in hand-to-hand combat with two large security guards, was zapped with a stun gun, was taken to a security room, was strapped to a chair, was mentally browbeaten, was hit across the face, and had to endure waterboarding as Carbone tried to find out what she knew.

Prior to 1932, the typical procedure was to report kidnappings to the local authorities. Kidnapping was considered a State crime.

After the kidnapping of the child of the famous aviator, Charles Lindbergh, the Federal Kidnapping Act was passed. This Act authorized the FBI to investigate kidnappings even when State lines were not crossed. The Act allowed the FBI to initiate a kidnapping investigation when a child of "tender years" was involved. This was first considered to apply to children under 12.

With a child abduction, typically the first report will be to the local police department. A missing persons' report will be filed. A request is then made for the child's name to be entered into the National Crime Information Center database. An Amber Alert is initiated.

To report a child abduction to the FBI, one reports to the local FBI field office, to the FBI Headquarters, or to the National Center for Missing and Exploited Children. The FBI Child Abduction Rapid Deployment team (CARD) may be deployed.

Typically, the FBI will not take over a case from local law enforcement, but will assist and pool resources with it.

Unfortunately, there are times when jurisdictional disputes between the police and the FBI interfere with progress. This is sometimes depicted in movies and on television. This type of conduct often become counter-productive as it detracts from the primary objective, saving the child's life and returning the child to his or her parents.

I was still at home. As evening set in, I became restless. Taylor told me where Moose lives, so I went there, uninvited. A stupid move, but I had become so full of stupid moves that they were all I had.

When I arrived at Moose's, I rang the doorbell. A woman who turned out to be Carol, Moose's wife, answered. I explained to her that I was a friend of Taylor's. She let me in. I am not certain whether Moose would have been so cordial.

I saw Moose. I asked him how he was progressing with raising his people. He was a little perturbed with me just showing up, but he had to let it go. Moose replied that he raised 12 people including himself and that they were going to meet at Smiley's at 1 a.m.

He explained that from Smiley's, it was only an hour or so to the compound and that the 1 a.m. departure time would provide the cover of darkness, a late hour for the compound guards, and plenty of time to disburse his people around the compound before sunrise.

Moose explained, "If Taylor is as smart as I hope she is, she will let on that she knows something so that it will be worth keeping her alive, at least for a couple of days.

"I have raised my biker army. I think Carbone has only four or five guards now. We can overwhelm them in fairly short order. Hopefully, they will realize that the girls are the only bargaining chip that they have so that it is in their best interest to keep them alive.

I asked Moose, "Is any of what you plan to do legal?"

As was his custom, Moose's response was quick and direct: "No."

I jumped in, "Then we will have no choice but to try for a citizen's arrest. When the time comes for you to speak directly to Carbone, I will let you know what needs to be said. For now, it will be necessary to contact the FBI as a citizen's arrest generally requires at least an attempt to involve the authorities."

Moose continued, "Actually, your FBI idea is not as stupid as some might think. Reporting criminal conduct to the FBI and being turned down for immediate help might actually give us some cover in the end."

CHAPTER 36

Assembly of the Biker Army

Before my arrival at Moose's house, he had hit the phones like a telemarketer on steroids. The rest of that evening and well into the night bikers began to arrive as Smiley's. It was a sight to behold. Chromed and tricked out hogs were line up in neat rows with guys so scary looking that it made me nervous, and they were on my side. They were getting ready for their 1 a.m. appointment.

Taylor was like a little sister to these guys. She was always there to help them with whatever they needed, and she never asked for anything in return. She did none of this for selfish reasons. I would seriously doubt that she ever thought that she would need to enlist anyone's help for anything, let alone to raise an army to save her life.

But loyalty and kindness freely given, at least today, was shown to be a great driver of people.

I do believe firmly that Carbone had finally met his match with her. Taylor demonstrated that personal loyalty is a great advantage. Let's see how loyal Carbone's people will be when push comes to shove. If I had to guess, I would say that they will cut and run and never look back. Some things money can't buy.

While at Moose's, my primary duty was to contact the FBI to let them know what we were doing. Even if I was ordered to do nothing, at least I could say that they were informed of the situation.

I asked Carol if I could use her phone. She said that I could.

The closest FBI field office was 400 miles away. I called. It was about 11 p.m., which was pretty late to be calling an office. I was hoping to be able to leave a message on their answering machine.

No such luck. The phone rang. A man answered, "FBI, may I help you?"

I replied, "Yes. I need to report a kidnapping. To whom should I speak?"

"You can speak to me. Everyone else went home hours ago. My name is Agent Alex Martinez."

"Yes, then, as I said, I would like to report a kidnapping."

"Let's start with your name."

"My name is Rick Miller."

"And what is your connection to the kidnapped person?"

"I teach at Newton Junior College. One of my students was the kidnapped person's babysitter. When the official kidnapping case went cold, she enlisted me to help her prove that the child was still alive."

"What is the name of the kidnap victim and the name of the babysitter?"

"The kidnap victim's name is Tammy Fitzgerald. The babysitter's name is Taylor Shaw."

"I think I remember this case. It was in all over the news. According to the local police department, the child was abducted and killed. There was a funeral. And the case has been long closed."

I said, "We have evidence that the child is still alive and is being held at the compound of Antony Carbone."

"Have you contacted the local authorities?"

"They, unfortunately, have been paid off by Carbone and have been working for him for years."

Agent Martinez replied, "You know you sound like a conspiracy nut. It is FBI protocol to not become directly involved in a kidnapping case without first contacting the local authorities. If we contact them, they will just tell us that the case is closed, and that will be the end of it."

I replied, "But we hiked up to the compound, and Taylor thought she saw Tammy."

"Well, let's talk to Taylor then."

"That would be great, but it appears as if she was caught snooping around and is also being held at the compound. If we don't do something quickly without Carbone knowing about it, I'm afraid both girls will be killed. Tammy is already thought to be dead, and Taylor comes from modest circumstances and will be labeled a teenage runaway and forgotten. Do you know this Carbone person?"

"Yes. Carbone is known. But we don't have enough on him to bring him in or to even talk to him about this. Kidnapping two girls is not really his style either. You know that if you report this to me, I will have no alternative but to contact the local police. They will probably tell us to mind our own business."

I said, "We have arranged to go to Carbone's to make a citizen's arrest. We need to move now. We cannot wait. The girls will be dead by tomorrow."

Agent Martinez, a little shaken, blurted out, "You can't do that. You will be breaking the law ten different ways and will wind up in jail yourself."

I thought to myself, every so often in life you have to do the right thing, regardless of the risks and the consequences. This was one of those times. I cannot sit by and let these two girls be slaughtered, even if this idiot can.

At this point, I trusted Moose more than the FBI and the local police, put together. I'd tell Moose to make his move as soon as possible. Without responding to the FBI's ridiculous evaluation, I hung up the phone. And may I tell you that if felt good.

CHAPTER 37

Moose Making it Happen

After I hung up the phone, it was time to leave for Smiley's. We reached Smileys just before 1 a.m. All of the men Moose enlisted were there. The time had come for Moose to get to the real business at hand, mapping out the logistics, and getting going already.

Moose rode his bike. I drove my car so that the girls would have transportation if we should be successful.

Moose and I parked and walked together towards the assembled men in the parking lot adjacent to Smiley's.

Before addressing the men, Moose asked me if I knew how many men Carbone had at the compound. I said that it appeared as if he had five or maybe six. One manned the guardhouse at the base of the private driveway. At least one acted as a rover. (This was probably the person who apprehended Taylor.) And three worked inside of the main house.

(It turned out that there were five, one in the guardhouse, one outside rover, and three inside of the main house.)

Moose said that his plan was to overwhelm them with sheer numbers. He had 11 guys plus himself ready to go. (For reasons too obvious to state, I was not counted.) His hope was that when Carbone discovered how outmanned he was, he would surrender, and they would not have to engage in much fighting. This was an ancient military trick.

In the *Art of War*, Sun Tzu famously said, "Supreme excellence consists of breaking the enemy's resistance without fighting." This was Moose's end game. Breaking Carbone and making him surrender without exposing the girls to a protracted gun battle in which they could be shot or worse in the cross-fire. As Carbone would certainly use the girls as human shields, it really made sense.

Watching the drone tape, I could see an old, dilapidated shack about 1000 yards into the unimproved area north of the compound. No one really knew about the shack as it could barely be seen from the compound. We needed to be careful to not leave much in the way of damage. Carbone could use damage as evidence that we threatened him physically.

Of Moose's 11 men, they all served, mostly in the army, and mostly in Desert Storm. Having served in the 1990's, the guys were a little older, which did not bother me.

I have always been a proponent of the theory that those who have served are much more adept at engaging in combat than those who have not. I believe that my theory has proven true when one looks at the last several Presidents.

Moose and I arrived at the group of assembled men. His plan was to address the men about the physical layout before heading out.

He said that the main public road leading up to the compound runs north with a ravine on one side and a 90-degree embankment on the other. Just before reaching the compound, the road turns east and runs along base of the hill below the front of the compound's main building.

One turns off of the main road at a flat area. This flat area leads to the start of the driveway running up to the compound.

There is a guardhouse at the beginning of the driveway manned by, it appeared, one guard from Carbone's staff.

As the driveway runs up the hill to the north towards the compound, it lists to the east. At the top of the driveway, there is a large motor court located on the east side of the main building. The front door for the main building opens into the motor court. During normal use, guests are dropped off in the motor court. Their vehicles are then taken to areas designated for parking north of the motor court.

The main house runs from east to west along the top of the hill. It is many feet higher than the main road and the beginning of the driveway below. All along the south side of the main house, there are windows with views to the south from which one may see the main road and far down into the valley below.

On the other, or north, side of the house, the rear yard is developed. In this developed area, there is a pool area and a tennis court. Beyond the developed portion, the property transitions into an unimproved area consisting of brush and earth ascending further to the north.

Moose explained to everyone that he was of the opinion that someone who is as well connected as Carbone would probably have his own private para-military group on call 24 hours a day. He would not trust his security to five or six rent-a-cops such as the security on duty at the main house.

Moose reasoned that if Carbone gets into trouble, he probably has a way of contacting his mercenaries by two-way radio which would be nearly impossible to jamb, even though all of the cellphones and video could and would be disabled.

Moose thought that the mercenaries would probably arrive by helicopter, as any other method would take too long.

He thought that they would probably land north of the improved property and filter down towards the compound. The unimproved portion of the site would provide a place to land, cover, and a convenient place from which to launch a guerilla-type assault, which Moose expected.

He thought that they would probably not land by the public road as they could easily be seen by anyone driving by.

Also, if they landed by the public road, they would have to fight their way up the hill, two miles, with no cover. If they landed on the unimproved area behind the house, they would be less than one mile from the house, would be moving downhill, and would have good cover.

Moose explained that we would stop along the main public road at a clearing well out of sight of the cut off to the driveway and guardhouse.

Moose's strategy was to send an advance team to check out the property and see if we could learn where the girls were being held. Another two men would take the guardhouse, replace the video feed with a loop, and place the guard or guards in custody away from the action. Any roving guard would also be apprehended and placed in the guardhouse. A flash drive would be made of the last 48 hours of video feed from both the grounds and the inside of the house for use as evidence later.

Moose delivered these final words to his men, "We need to remember that unlike us, Carbone is not a soldier; he is a murderer. As such, he will not be playing by any rules or following any standards of human conduct. This means that all people, non-combatants, women, and children, will be considered to be fair game. This means that you will have to proceed with caution with this guy. Our mission is to rescue the two girls alive and nothing else. We are not fighting a war. It is not our duty to send a message to the other side, or to anyone else for that matter. If Carbone does unleash a para-military group against us, it is our mission to capture and confine the combatants for the duration of this engagement. The same goes for Carbone and his immediate security guard detail. Let's go now and get these two girls out of there alive."

His words were riveting. It was not unlike a coach giving a pep-talk to his team before a big game.

We took off from Smiley's. A contingent of 12 tricked out motorcycles each manned with an ex-military special-forces person and multiple weapons. Moose was in the lead. As I watched, I could only think of the scene in Easy Rider in which the main characters take off on their motorcycles as the Steppenwolf song plays in the background.

The group arrived near the compound around 2:00 a.m. It was still dark. We parked along the main public road at a clearing well out of site of the guardhouse.

Moose dispatched the communications guy and another of his people to the guardhouse. They made short work of the guard. He was disabled, tied up, and locked in a closet in the guardhouse.

Our communications guy was one of the best in the world (the very best in the entire world, according to Moose).

He made quick work of the security system, which he called very rudimentary. Others might disagree, but his experience was with the most sophisticated equipment in the world. He produced a flash drive of the past 48 hours, and secured it for later.

He used a wireless jammer, specifically a 2.4 GHz jamming device. This would jam the signal from the cameras and all of the phones. Carbone would be left unable to call for help, unless the call was via a private two-way radio which could not be jammed.

The monitors within the compound would be reprogrammed to see only a continuous image of the road, the driveway, the house, the outbuildings, and all of the other images customarily appearing on the monitors' screens. The entire system would be disabled from photographing anything. In other words, after we left there would be no video or photographic evidence of anything. The entire system would be crashed. The only thing remaining would be the flash drive that we produced when we arrived, and we would have possession of it.

The lead team apprehended the roving guard. They captured him, tied him up, and put him in the closet in the guardhouse with the guard from the guardhouse so quickly and quietly that you barely knew it happened.

After clearing the two outside guards, Carbone, unbeknownst to him, would be left with only the three inside guards.

As to the main house, we knew that the front door was on the east. It was presumed that Carbone's private office was near the front door probably on the south, as the south had the view of the valley.

The north looked to the pool, tennis court, and the unimproved land beyond. From my prior excursion to the property, we knew that Tammy was kept in private quarters on the far west side of the house, a location relatively far from Carbone's office and the front door. Her private yard was north outside of the west side of the house.

A man from the advance team made his way around to the west side of the house behind the private yard. Using an infrared viewer, he was of the opinion that there were two people in the far west room. One appeared to be holding the other person hostage. Moose presumed that this is where Taylor was being kept by one of the security guards.

He reasoned that Carbone felt that he needed to separate the two girls as the little girl was probably becoming agitated and difficult when Taylor was present. Killing Taylor was of no consequence to him. He could always say that he caught her breaking in. However, he needed to be much more careful with Tammy. It was obvious that she did not break in, and killing her would be difficult, if not impossible, to explain away. (It also might cause Don to pull out of the casino project.) He needed to keep her close to him.

We need to keep in mind that everyone on Moose's team was connected with coms. As military men, they knew that communication was the key to a successful mission. The guards, on the other hand, had no way of communicating with one another, except by yelling.

Learning that at least one of the girls appeared to be held in the west room, Moose made the first of the many bold moves that he would make that day.

He ordered Bart to move to the west side, enter the compound, enter the building, and take the hostage back. This was to be done without anyone else in the house knowing about it. Neat trick if you can find someone with the skill to do it, and Moose knew that Bart was just that someone.

I was tapped to accompany him, as I knew how to get to the west side and where the fence was located. Bart is the person who instructed Taylor in hand-to-hand combat on their camping trip.

Inside of the west room Taylor was, in fact, being held by a single security guard. She was tied up. Seeing that she was attractive, the security guard was attempting to have his way with her. She was not having any of it. He finally got frustrated and pulled a knife.

By this time, Bart and I had reached the electric fence. I showed him the opening in the fence where Taylor entered the property. He studied the fence with an amused look on his face. He grounded and shorted out the fence, cut a hole in it, and was at the door to the west side of the house within minutes.

The door was locked. He picked the lock and opened the door faster than I could open it with a key. We entered a common hallway. The first door on the left was for the room where Taylor was being held.

We could hear Taylor vocally rebuffing the guard's advances. I started to really become unhinged. Bart calmed me down. He told me that engaging in combat is similar to playing a competitive sport. If you cannot control yourself, you will never be able to control your opponent. That settled me down.

I didn't know how he was going to gain access to the room without alerting the rest of the people in the house, and here is what he did.

He knocked gently on the door. This immediately stopped the attempted rape because the security guard had to pause to see who was at the door.

In a muffled voice he said, "Got coffee and a bear claw for you." (Who thinks of something like that under this pressure?)

Whether he recognized the voice or not, the guard had to open the door to see who it was.

When the door was opened I swear just one millimeter, Bart burst his left hand through the crack and grabbed the guard by the throat with such force that it paralyzed his vocal chords (and almost killed him).

He was careful to not beat him too badly as Moose instructed everyone to leave the prisoners in relatively good physical shape. (It would have been such fun to watch him really do a number on this a-hole.)

Taylor ran over to us and put her arms around me. I was thinking to myself that I had little to do with what just transpired, but I was there for her.

Bart tied up the guard, and we took him back through the fence and over to the guardhouse where he joined the other two guards.

Carbone was now down to two guards in the house.

Our entire group of 12 men including Moose along with me and Taylor gathered near the guardhouse.

Moose said that he was going to divide us into two groups. The larger group would move past the motor court, past the improved part of the property, and into the unimproved foothills behind the property to the north.

The smaller group, including him, would move to the east side of the motor court opposite the front door.

Moose instructed the group moving to the north to begin setting traps including digging holes and covering them with brush to capture anyone who fell in, arming bear traps, and setting out any other contraptions of which they could think. He seemed to be fairly certain that Carbone would have a para-military group and that the group would attack from the north. (He proved to be correct on both counts. No surprise.)

Prisoners caught in traps or subdued by hand-to-hand combat would be tied up and taken to the shed in the foothills.

Moose would let them know when to assemble the captives in the shed and in the guardhouse and bring them to the motor court. He would then present them to Carbone and try to talk him into surrendering.

Just a footnote. When Moose spoke, it was not a negotiation, and everyone present knew it. Whatever he said to do was done, immediately. There would be no alternate plans considered, and talking back could be the speaker's last bit of communication on this earth. In the military, orders were orders, and they were obeyed without question. Moose asked Bart to return to the west side entrance and await instructions. He told us that he might want Bart to again infiltrate the building to retrieve Tammy.

Taylor insisted on going with Bart on this mission. Moose balked, as one would expect.

Taylor told Moose that the house was very large and intricate and that Bart might have trouble finding his way from the west side entrance to Tammy's location without her. She told Moose that she knew the house fairly well as she had been moved around to several rooms during her imprisonment the day before.

I really think that she just felt that it was necessary for her to be part of Tammy's advance team if Moose needed Bart to breach to rescue Tammy.

Moose uncharacteristically relented. I would go with them but would probably not enter the house unless needed.

The larger group moved to the north side of the property. They began setting elaborate traps and finding places to take cover. If Carbone sent a para-military group, they would never see Moose's men coming.

Bart, Taylor, and I moved around to the west on the trail that by now we knew only too well. We huddled near the disabled electric fence to await Moose's orders.

Moose and his group moved to their location at the edge of the motor court opposite the front door. From this location, Moose would make his initial contact with Carbone.

When Moose and I first arrived at the compound, I told him that in order for us be able to contend that we were acting legally, we needed to make it appear as if we there to make a citizen's arrest. I explained that under PC 837 a citizen's arrest could be made if the citizen knows either directly or indirectly that the perpetrator committed a felony. With the captive status of both Tammy and Taylor being known, Moose certainly had knowledge of the commission of a felony.

I told Moose that it would be important for him to inform Carbone that it was his intent to arrest him. I told Moose that it would be necessary for him to clearly state the cause of the arrest, his authority to make the arrest, and that he informed law enforcement of his intention to make the arrest, which we did.

Over the bullhorn, Moose carefully crafted this message: "Antony Carbone, this is Giovanni Moustaka. I am a retired Army Ranger. I have men with me here at this compound, but do not intend to harm you. Our intent here today is to make a citizen's arrest of you for holding Tammy Fitzgerald and Taylor Shaw within your compound against their will. Our authority to make this arrest is that we are concerned for the safety of these two people. We have called the authorities to inform them of the situation. Please be so kind as to release the two young ladies to us. When they are safely with us, we will depart from these premises, and no harm will come to you or your men."

"If the two young ladies are not returned to us shortly, we will have no alternative but to enter the building and retrieve them. We will make every effort to leave you, your staff, and your property undamaged.

"Please let us know when the ladies will be released."

Carbone, ever the idiot-optimist, yelled his reply through the front door, "Johnny, or whatever your name is, I have just sent a message to my military people. They will be arriving here by helicopter within a couple of minutes. They will kill you and your rag-tag team of so-called army veterans."

In a flash, with this bold, yet very stupid, statement, all bets were, as they say, off. (Carbone may be accused of many things, but being smart will not be one of them.)

Just then the telltale cutting of helicopter blades through the air could be heard coming over the hill from the north. The craft landed in a clearing which could not be seen from the house or from the motor court.

Moose spoke with his man Hector on the satellite phone. He said, "Hector, wait until everyone exits and clears the chopper."

Hector replied, "And then what boss?"

Moose said, "Once everyone has cleared the chopper, blow it to bits."

Hector's reply was short and succinct, "Yes, sir."

Why you ask? Moose knew that when Carbone's hired army saw their chopper was blown to bits that they would no longer have a comfortable escape route.

With the chopper blown up, they would know that their only alternative was to stay and fight, perhaps to the death. This might cause them to think twice about what they were doing.

They might have been willing to land their chopper as a show of force, but were they willing to fight and die for Carbone? With no escape route, they knew that fighting was their only alternative. It was a terrific psychological ploy.

After Carbone's men cleared the chopper, Hector unleased a surface to surface missile against it. What was once a helicopter was reduced to a pile of metal rubble scattered around the countryside, with parts still on fire. Though the blast could be heard, it was too far away to be seen. Carbone, thinking that his men released the blast, yelled to Moose, "You see, your men are already taking fire."

The destruction of the helicopter left Carbone's men with only one option, the option of fighting. They started moving south towards the compound to engage Moose, having been told by Carbone, incorrectly, that Moose and the majority of his men were at the motor court just opposite the front door.

They were not aware that most of Moose's men were actually in the brush between the landing site and the motor court, the type of terrain well suited for Moose's team.

Carbone's team initially consisted of 12 men. Two men fell into the hole in the ground trap. They were bound, gagged, and taken to the shed where they were held.

One man stepped into the rope trap and was hoisted, upside down, and left hanging from a tree branch. He was also bound, gagged, and taken to the shed.

It was not going to be as easy as marching down to the motor court and engaging Moose's men directly. They could see that Moose's men were scattered and hidden in the brush. In their way of thinking, they were going to have to separate and go into the brush after them, as was customary in guerilla warfare. This proved to be a grave tactical error, as it allowed Moose's men to isolate the enemy.

Two of Carbone's men moved to the west and were out of site from the rest of the group. Nick, a desert storm vet, grabbed both of them, beat them, gagged them, and brought them to the shed.

Another of Carbone's men made the fatal mistake of taking off alone in a frustrated effort to find someone to shoot. Unfortunately for him, he selected Lester.

Moose's man Lester, the gun specialist, popped out from behind a tree causing Carbone's guy to pursue. Snap. One of the bear traps caught his foot and leg, cutting deeply into his skin. He cried in pain. Showing some mercy, Lester extricated him from the trap, gagged him, and carried him to the shed. It would be a while before he would be doing any walking on his own accord.

Carbone was getting the sinking feeling that Moose was engaging his men in the brush to the north and not allowing them to reach the compound proper, which was true.

Two of Carbone's men made the mistake of circling around to the west thinking that they could flank Moose's people. They ran into another very unfortunate fate. They ran into Bart.

At this point Bart was not pleased with Carbone or his people. Bart beat these two poor guys to a pulp before tying them up, which, in their condition, was barely necessary. We found a place for them near the fence, and I was assigned the task of staying with them until it was time to take them to the guardhouse to be placed with the other captives.

Hector and his team engaged the remaining four men in hand-to-hand combat. I heard that it was like something out of the movies. Eight men fighting with vicious techniques. Ultimately, Moose's men subdued them and took them to the shed.

Carbone, not pleased, yelled at Moose, "You see my men have completely defeated your little group. Now get out of here."

Carbone really lived in a dream world.

Moose knew that Carbone would be livid when he learned that his entire team had been captured and that Taylor had already been rescued. Moose was afraid that he might do something stupid with respect to Tammy.

Moose felt it was time to have Bart infiltrate the house to retrieve Tammy. Bart and Taylor entered through the west side door. Taylor was right. It was a maze of hallways and rooms.

Taylor was of the opinion that Tammy would probably be held in the security room, as it was adjacent to Carbone's private office and was equipped to handle a captive. Taylor and Bart moved through the center hall. Taylor motioned for them to enter the meeting room. It was on the south side of the hall and was on the other side of the wall from the security room.

They entered the meeting room. There was a door between it and the security room allowing one to move from one room to the other without going back into the main hallway. This was good. If they had to enter the security room from the hall, they would certainly have been seen by Carbone.

Bart reasoned that if a guard was holding Tammy, because of all of the commotion, he would be very close to her. Bart thought that if the guard saw him first, he would not have sufficient time to disable him before he could hurt Tammy badly.

He told Taylor that he had a plan but that his plan was risky. He told her that he would understand if she did not want to participate. Taylor's reply, of course, was no way, whatever you think we should do, I will do.

Bart's plan was for Taylor to enter the security room by herself and allow the guard to see her. The guard would be surprised because Taylor was supposed to be being held in another room in another part of the house.

Bart reasoned that this moment of surprise and movement of the guard away from Tammy to apprehend Taylor might provide just enough time for him to grab and disable the guard before he could hurt Tammy.

Taylor entered the security room, putting herself into the plain sight of the guard holding Tammy. The guard, knowing that he needed to capture Taylor too, was forced to move away from Tammy to do so.

In that split second when he let go of Tammy to apprehend Taylor, Bart moved on the guard, grabbing him by the throat. Bart grabbed him so tightly that the guard almost perished.

As with the other guard, he paralyzed his vocal chords so he could not warn Carbone. At that point, Carbone was so wrapped up with his own trouble at the front door that he might not have noticed the guard's capture even if he had been able to scream.

Bart and Taylor quietly moved Tammy and the newly captured guard out through the west door. This was one time when having a house that was a little too large worked against him. The house was so vast that one could move around in it without being seen or heard in other parts of the house.

Taylor, Bart, Tammy, and I hiked down the hill to the guardhouse bringing the two para-military types that Bart apprehended on the west side of the property and the security guard that he just apprehended while freeing Tammy.

The two para-military types and the security guard who was guarding Tammy were brought to the guardhouse where they were added to the security guard who was guarding Taylor, the security guard who manned the guardhouse, and the security guard who had been the roamer for a total of six people.

Hector was holding the 10 para-military types who had been captured in the shed.

Bart brought his six captives and Hector brought his 10 captives to the east side of the motor court where Moose was located. The total of 16 men were chained together and placed on the east side of the motor court in plain view of Carbone and the front door of the house. He had Taylor and Tammy in a nearby safe location which was also in plain view of Carbone and the front door.

Using the bullhorn, Moose addressed Carbone as follows, "As you may see, we now have Taylor and Tammy in our custody. We have captured your entire para-military staff and four of your five security guards. The one remaining security guard is with you at the front door now. We intend to leave these premises now. We will leave your para-military personnel and the four security guards chained together and locked to the fence in the motor court where you see them now. Please offer no further resistance, as it will be futile."

Moose, his men, Taylor, Tammy, and I moved down the driveway and to our respective modes of transportation.

While walking down the driveway, I said to Moose, "I cannot thank you enough for everything you and your people did here today. I would really have been lost, and the authorities did not seem too interested in helping."

I then addressed Taylor, "Taylor, it is so great to see you."

Taylor hugged me hard for a long time and said, "Oh, Rick, you have been so great to me. Besides you and Moose and his people, all of the men in my life have been such a tremendous disappointment. Thank you."

I ask Taylor, "And this must be Tammy?"

Taylor replied, "Yes."

Tammy was not in very good shape. She really needed medical care. Months of poor treatment and nutrition. Should we take her directly to the hospital? Should we take her home? She appeared to be suffering from malnutrition. And there would be years of therapy.

As the men reached their motorcycles, Taylor, Tammy, and I made it to my car. Taylor and Tammy got into the back seat. Tammy curled up in Taylor's arms and gently cried. We were starting our trip back to Newton.

I figured I would let Taylor make the decision about where we would take Tammy. It occurred to me that Tammy did not know about her father's involvement with her kidnapping. Maybe it would be better if it stayed that way, at least for now.

I didn't want to ask Taylor about her time with Carbone. I thought it might upset her and Tammy, and me too for that matter. Besides, Taylor and I would have plenty of time to talk about everything that went on when Tammy was either in a hospital or with her mother.

I turned the car onto the main road and headed back towards the interstate.

I asked, "Where are we off to?"

Taylor replied, "Don and Diane's house."

Simple enough.

CHAPTER 38

Don and Diane's House

I drove. The girls remained huddled in the back seat. Tammy cried all of the way home while Taylor held and comforted her. Oh, to have a friend like that.

We arrived at Haven Lakes. We reached the first guard gate, the gate for the subdivision. I stopped. The upper portion of the Dutch door was open.

The guard asked, "Who are you here to see?"

I responded, "Mr. and Mrs. Fitzgerald."

"No name was left here. I'll need to call. Who are you?"

"My name is Rick Miller, but they don't know me. I have their daughter, Tammy, in my car along with her babysitter, Taylor Shaw." The guard telephoned the house. After a short conversation he said, "Please go ahead to the next guard gate."

We arrived at the next guard gate, the gate for the section with the larger houses, including the Fitzgerald house. When the guard saw us, he opened the gate and motioned for us to go through. He must have heard from the Fitzgerald residence.

I entered the section. Taylor told me to go straight, take a right, go to the end of the road, and take a left. The house would be the last house at the end of the cul-de-sac, the house furthest to the rear of all of the houses in both the regular subdivision and the portion of the subdivision with the large houses.

We came up to the house. It was a mansion overshadowing even the other large houses. It was set back 50 feet from the street, had an imposing front façade, and a huge rear yard with a swimming pool, spa, tennis court, barbecue, guesthouse, and sitting area.

Taylor asked me to drive up the driveway.

As we drove up to the house, Diane, followed by Don, came running out. Jason was away at school.

Taylor helped Tammy out of the car. Diane grabbed her and began hugging her. Tammy renewed her crying. But these were cries of joy at being in the arms of her mother.

Whatever went on between Tammy and Diane before Tammy's kidnapping was now long forgotten. We can only hope that lessons learned will make the relationship stronger going forward.

Remember that at this point, Tammy did not know of her father's involvement with Carbone and her kidnapping. She threw her arms around him. He, though a little stiff, tried his best to return the gesture and to not show any signs of his complicity.

It was now clear. When the family first learned of the abduction, Diane became delirious with grief, whereas Don seemed a little reserved.

At that point, though Don was unhappy, he had the comfort of knowing that Tammy was still alive. Diane did not have that luxury. As far as she knew, Tammy was kidnapped and killed. If ever questioned about it, Don could pass it off as the difference between the way men and women process grief.

Watching all of this unfold, I have to say that Taylor showed great restraint in not confronting Don (or worse, beating him up right there on the spot which she certainly could have done and which certainly would have been warranted).

We would talk about it later, but I figured that it was still to be decided whether it would be better to tell Tammy about her father's involvement or to hide it. If she told Tammy, Diane would certainly leave Don, and Tammy would be left with in a broken home. (That's assuming that Diane did not strangle him herself.)

Diane spoke to Taylor and Tammy, "How did this happen? How are you still alive? The police gave up on this case long ago."

Taylor replied, "I never believed that Tammy was dead. When I started looking into the case, there were many inconsistencies, and the police work was subpar. I had gone down all of the roads that a 19-year-old girl could go down. A 19-year-old from modest circumstances with no money, no job, and no family connections could easily be marginalized, which I was when I tried to investigate by myself.

"Then one day, Mr. Miller here, showed up to teach a class in which I was enrolled. He told us that he was a lawyer and had worked in criminal prosecution in the DA's office. From his first lecture, I could see that he was a little more objective than most of the men I knew.

"I felt that with his education, he might be open to new ideas and that he wouldn't classify people like me based on my age and gender, the way most adults do. He seemed to be someone who might understand.

"I was bold. I asked him for his help. He met me, and to my surprise, he listened. Rather than just saying that I was crazy, he really seemed to care and seemed genuinely interested in helping me. It was difficult at first, but as we got further into the case, things began to take shape."

Diane turned to me and said, "Then, thank you, Mr. Miller, for all of your help."

I replied, "It was my pleasure. But I need to confess that my interest, at least at first, was not purely altruistic. Ms. Shaw here is quite enchanting, as I am sure you can see."

Diane then said to me, "Well, that's okay. Attraction can be a great motivator. I'm just happy that it got done."

Diane then turned to Taylor and thinking that I could not hear her said, "He's also pretty easy on the eyes, Miss Shaw."

Taylor blushed.

We bid our farewell to the group. There would be much conversation between Taylor and me as to how to handle things going forward, but not tonight. I drove towards Taylor's mom's house. I said, "I'll take you home. I'm sure that after your ordeal you would like to take a shower and get some sleep."

She nodded in agreement and said, "But I hope I can see you tomorrow."

I told her that she could see me any time she wished, and that her well-being is, and has always been, my primary concern. She told me about the treatment she received at Carbone's, the slapping and the waterboarding. She told me that she would not tell them who else knew about Tammy, which seemed to make them even more agitated. As it was getting late and they were making no progress, they agreed to take up the rest of the waterboarding the next morning. Fortunately, Moose showed up before they could get started.

Taylor's loyalty never ceased to amaze me. Here is a person who grew up with practically nothing. No father. A mother who was drunk most of the time, including when she was entertaining some really awful people. But she wouldn't abandon her mother, even though her mother basically abandoned her.

I dropped Taylor off and went home. It was now nighttime.

I slept well, for a change. At 9 a.m. my phone rang. I answered. On the other end of the line I heard:

"Mr. Miller please."

I replied, "This is he."

The caller continued, "This is Agent Martinez of the FBI. We spoke a couple of days ago about Antony Carbone."

"I remember."

"We heard that you went to Mr. Carbone's house and threatened him."

"That's not true. We went there to make a citizen's arrest. Mr. Moustaka, our spokesman, along with everyone in the free world, knew that Carbone committed multiple felonies by holding Tammy Fitzgerald and Taylor Shaw captive without their consent. Mr. Moustaka advised Mr. Carbone of our intent to arrest him, the cause of his arrest, our authority to make the arrest, and the fact that we notified the authorities, namely you. So, he decided to give us Taylor and Tammy."

Mr. Martinez continued, "The local police might take exception to that characterization of the events. And I suppose he just gave them to you out of the goodness of his heart, with no threat of violence?"

"Firstly, I don't know how they can take exception to my characterization of the events seeing that they were not there. As to Carbone, yes one could say that he gave us the girls out of the kindness of his heard."

"And why would he do that?"

"He must have had a crisis of conscience."

"He said you destroyed his com system."

"That would be impossible. You would need the most experienced com person in the world to begin to work on a system as advanced as his." (Little did he know that we had the most experienced com person in the world who really did disable the thing, perhaps beyond repair.)

Agent Martinez continued, "Taylor was not kidnapped. She was caught trespassing."

I replied, "If you are really that gullible, I presume that you will believe what you wish. In fact, she was attempting to collect evidence to establish probable cause for a search warrant. This was obviously impossible from the street which is over a mile away from the compound. She hiked up the hillside through unimproved land. There is no way of knowing whether this property belonged to Carbone or not without a surveyor.

"As we both know, whatever a private citizen uncovers through his or her search is admissible in court, even if the search is illegal."

Martinez interjected, "Mr. Carbone categorically denies that he tortured or even laid a hand on Ms. Shaw."

"And I presume that you and your FBI friends know what a terrific reputation Mr. Carbone has for telling the truth. Besides, we have it all on video."

Agent Martinez, who was becoming a real bore, continued, "And Mr. Carbone says that Tammy was left in his care by her father and was not kidnapped at all."

I finished our conversation with this, "You are either the most stupid or the most dishonest FBI agent in the entire agency, no offense. It seems as if you have us blocked from every angle: Tammy was not kidnapped at all, even though she was kept at a strange man's compound without being allowed to leave for a long time. You say that Taylor was trespassing. Even if she was trespassing, that would never justify Carbone having her beaten up, tortured, and held over-night. If those are your theories, you must be insane or just plain stupid."

I concluded with, "You apparently have no interest in going after Carbone or the Haven-Newton Police Department, which has been enabling Carbone for years. It seems as if you are more interested in pressuring me and Taylor to drop our investigation and give up our rights than pursuing the actual crimes and civil wrongs that were committed. Anyway, I will leave it there for now. Bye."

I hung up. I was a little disappointed, but not surprised. Carbone had bought himself another stooge, and this stooge was in the FBI.

CHAPTER 39
Reporting to Taylor

It was now around 9:30, and I didn't want to call Taylor until 10. It occurred to me that I had not collected the mail from the previous couple of days.

I went to the mailbox. In the mailbox, among other letters, was a large, flat envelope from the DNA testing lab. I opened it. In it, there was a DNA report. I read over the first few paragraphs of the report.

The report stated that though there was initially no match to the DNA we sent, it appears as if since that time, a match was found. The report stated that after we submitted our DNA sample, there was an automobile accident which claimed the life of one José Luis Valdez.

Apparently, the vehicle he was driving went over a cliff and plunged into a deep ravine. He died, and his remains were found. As the deceased could not be identified, dental records were used and DNA was gathered for the purpose of identifying him.

After using his dental records and DNA to identify him, as a matter of procedure, Mr. Valdez's DNA was added to CODIS. When this was done, it triggered a match to the DNA we submitted, the DNA collected from Tammy's room.

In short, the DNA collected from Tammy's room was found to be a match to the DNA belonging to José Luis Valdez. It just so happened that Mr. Valdez was Mr. Fitzgerald's gardener.

It appears as if Mr. Fitzgerald's gardener may have been the kidnapper.

It was now coming up on 10 a.m., and I felt I could call Taylor.

Groggy, as if awakened from a deep sleep, Taylor answered, "Hello?"

"Hi, it's Rick. Did I awaken you? You must be trashed."

"No. I need to get up anyway."

"I wanted to tell you about some of the things I have found out about the case."

"Anything good?" Taylor asked.

"No. Not really," I replied.

"Go ahead then."

"I spoke with Agent Martinez, the FBI guy. He said that we threatened violence against Mr. Carbone and could be prosecuted.

"He said that Tammy was not kidnapped, but was allowed to stay with Mr. Carbone by her father. He said that your actions snooping around Carbone's compound amounted to trespassing. He said that the FBI had no interest in investigating the Haven-Newton Police Department or in pursuing any other conspiracy theory.

"Also, I received in the mail a report from our DNA lab. The report states that when they collected DNA from Tammy's room and entered it into CODIS, there were no matches, as we knew.

Subsequently, however, there was a suspicious automobile death. As a matter of routine, the decedent's DNA was entered into CODIS. When this was done, our lab was notified that the newly entered DNA was a match to the DNA we submitted.

"The victim of the suspicious death was José Luis Valdez, Mr. Fitzgerald's gardener. It appears as if Mr. Valdez may have entered Tammy's room and kidnapped her."

"I see," Taylor said. "They seem to have blocked us at every turn. Well, that's too bad for us. But the human cost of pursuing the case could be great."

Taylor made the kind of case only she could make. "At this point, Tammy knows that she was kidnapped and that no one, except us, made a real effort to find her. This is painful and will probably haunt her for the rest of her life. But with therapy and people who care about her to talk to, she has a chance at a normal life.

"If we tell Tammy that she was kidnapped with the knowledge of her father, or if her father is prosecuted for his part in the kidnapping, she may or may not believe it. But whether she believes it or not, on some level, it will forever damage their relationship.

"Diane can either deny that there was a kidnapping and remain married to Don or prosecute Don and Carbone, divorce Don, and become a single mom with two children and no job.

"As to my snooping, it was probably technically trespassing. I doubt that Carbone would spend the time and energy necessary to pursue it as an independent case, but he could certainly use it as a counterclaim if we pursue him.

"The fact that this FBI agent does not want to pursue the Haven-Newton Police Department does not surprise me. Carbone has bought everyone else, why not him? To go this route, we would have to find an honest FBI agent at a different field office, but there would be no guarantee of success.

"As to the DNA, that was a stroke of genius. At the time of the kidnapping, Carbone knew that the gardener was an illegal immigrant and would not have DNA on file. Because of this, he did not have to worry that the DNA being collected at the crime scene might point to him or even to anyone who might be identifiable. This is why the DNA collection was such a non-issue at the time it was collected.

"Carbone had the gardener contact Mr. Fitzgerald by telephone to tell him that he had kidnapped his daughter and that Carbone would keep her until he came through with permission for the casino project.

"The phone records would only show a call from a gardener to his customer, nothing out of the ordinary. Carbone could get Don the message without the call being traced back to him. Additionally, the gardener could return to the crime scene the next day and clean up any evidence he might have left because it was his job to be there cleaning up.

"After the passage of a few months, Carbone could have the gardener killed, and no one would know the difference. And this is exactly what would have happened if we had not gathered the touch DNA evidence and submitted it to the lab for testing and addition to CODIS.

"What makes me mad is that I should have known by the way Mr. Fitzgerald was acting at the funeral that something was not right. I should have known that he seemed a little too relaxed.

And now we know it was because even then he knew that Tammy was safe, and he didn't care if she was inconvenienced."

"I think you did know," was all that I could say.

Taylor asked, "What about us? I've been really unfair with you throughout this ordeal. You've given a lot of your time and taken some major risks for me, and I have not really been there for you."

I replied, "My concern is that after the resolution of the kidnapping you might no longer have a reason to hang out with me. Face facts, if you really liked me, we would have been together over these past months, regardless of what was going on with the case. Being with someone just because you are helping them out is really the same as not being with them at all.

"Please believe me when I say that I'm not mad or even disappointed. I'm just trying to be realistic. You are young and beautiful and have many options before you. I'm always going to be around for you."

Taylor closed, "I understand."

Whether Taylor and I ever succeed in having a real relationship is not important. I like to think that we will, and I like to think that we could team up to take on the world and whatever it throws at us.

Right now, she is only 19 and does not really know what she will be doing in the future. I'm 29, have finished school, and have been working in a career job for several years. I'm ready to settle down. She is not.

But the important takeaway is this: Loyalty - Taylor's, Moose's, and even mine, triumphed over greed. Valuable lessons were learned.

Over the next several weeks, Taylor and I will have to decide where we go from here with everything we have learned about Carbone, Don Fitzgerald, the Haven-Newton Police Department, and the local FBI.

CHAPTER 40

Where We Go From Here

Taylor and I did not speak for a few days, as I anticipated. Nothing bad. We were both busy. I finished my teaching duties thereby fulfilling my contract. I would now be free to return to my job in Haven.

Taylor was busy with school, and she would have quite a bit still ahead. She only completed a little over one semester so far and would likely have three and a half more years of undergraduate school and then graduate school.

She finally contacted me and wanted to get together. We met at my office on campus. Secrecy was no longer an issue, and going all the way out to Smiley's seemed to be a waste of time at this point.

I heard her at the door. "Come in."

She entered the room. "May I sit."

"Of course."

When she began speaking, I knew right away that it was just about the case and not about us, but that's okay.

I listened to her, which in her way of thinking is very important.

She started, "Are we satisfied with the outcome of all we went through to find Tammy and bring her home? Are we okay with the fact that it appears as if Don and Carbone may get off scot-free after all of the horrible things they did to Tammy and to me too for that matter? Are we okay with the Haven-Newton Police Department and the local FBI office being allowed to continue, business as usual, with no consequences for being bought and paid for by a notorious gangster?"

Keeping it all business, I replied, "Very good questions. I've been thinking about all of this too. You know, that in addition to all of the things that Don and Carbone did in furtherance of the kidnapping, they also swindled many home owners and defrauded several lenders when they worked together before the kidnapping and the building of Haven Lakes.

"You always implied that you had an interest in the law. What would you say if we analyze the facts and see if pursuing Carbone, Don, and the others makes any sense from a legal standpoint?"

She seemed agreeable, so I continued: "In any legal analysis, we start with the facts. Some of the facts will not be disputed, but others will. Each side will present the facts as it sees them and will be asked to prove his or her version of the facts with admissible evidence.

"We know that Tammy was taken from her home and remained missing for quite a while. We learned that she was being held at Carbone's compound. These facts we can prove.

"We believe that Carbone was holding the girl against her will to persuade her father to work harder at getting permission to build his casino project.

"The other side will dispute the fact that Tammy was being held against her will or that she was being held to persuade her father to do anything. Further, they will say that her father allowed her to stay at Carbone's compound and that she was living there with his consent.

"We will have to show that Tammy's mother did not know that Tammy was alive and that she did not consent to Tammy living at Carbone's. This may require Diane to testify against her husband. Here, we might run into the spousal privilege but that would probably not apply in a situation where one is charged with a crime against the child of the other.

"With respect to you, we will have to show that you innocently hiked up the hill to gather evidence for a search warrant. We will have to show that you were attacked, beaten, and tasered. We will have to show that you were taken to a private room, verbally brow-beaten, physically struck across the face, and waterboarded. This will all be denied by Carbone and his guards.

"I believe that one of our best legal plays is to emphasize the torture. Assault and battery without severe damage will not carry penalties as heavy as one might think; however, torture will. Torture can get a person life in prison without the possibility of parole.

"Moose told me that his com guy made a flash drive of Carbone's security tapes for 48 hours before our arrival. This would include video evidence of you being tortured. This will be of great value in your case, as the torture would otherwise be denied and would be difficult to prove.

"If one of the security guards did not directly participate in the torture, we might be able to persuade him to testify against Carbone for a reduced sentence.

"As to Moose, we will have to show that the methods he used were lawful as a citizen's arrest under PC 837. We have a record that the FBI was asked for help before self-help was initiated.

"Under PC 837, to make a citizen's arrest, the citizen must either know or have reasonable cause to believe that a crime was committed. I think that the holding of you and Tammy made that pretty obvious.

"The citizen needs to inform the person that he intends to arrest him, set forth the cause of the arrest, indicate his authority to make the arrest, and inform the him that he contacted the authorities."

"I explained this to Moose, and I believe that he told all of this to Carbone during his initial bullhorn warning. It was Carbone who rejected his offer and countered with his para-military strike team.

"As to the law generally, when a person acts very badly, his conduct may be considered a crime. The State will prosecute the perpetrator as it has an interest in protecting the people of the State from criminal conduct, whether the victim agrees or not.

"If the conduct is less bad but is still unacceptable, rather than a crime, the conduct may be considered a tort. Torts are not prosecuted by the State but give the injured party the right to sue the actor for monetary damages in civil court.

"The same conduct may be both a crime and a tort. If it a crime, it may be considered a misdemeanor or a felony depending on the seriousness of the transgression. This is known as a wobbler.

"A distinction worth noting is that in a criminal case, the State must prove its case beyond a reasonable doubt. In a civil case, the injured party must only prove his case by the preponderance of the evidence.

"Because of the different burdens of proof, a guilty verdict in a criminal case might conclusively prove liability in a civil case whereas a finding of liability in a civil case would not necessarily prove guilt in a criminal case.

"Often in a criminal case, the primary charge has lesser included offenses. In this case, kidnapping typically includes the lesser offense of false imprisonment. Because a child was involved, we also have a possible violation of the child abduction law.

"With the facts we have, in addition to kidnapping and its related offenses, we have assault and battery, which may be both criminal and civil. We also have torture, which is criminal.

"Also, we have the real estate swindles and fraudulent loan transactions in which Don and Carbone engaged for a couple of years to throw into the mix."

"Further, we have misconduct by the Haven-Newton Police Department which might give rise to a Department of Justice investigation.

Taylor was spell-bound. She said, "Wow. This is all so interesting. Maybe I should go to law school. We can work together to solve cases."

"I think you would make a great lawyer. You think things through and are not afraid to speak your mind."

I side-stepped the working together part of her statement.

I continued, "Getting back to the case, kidnapping would be an obvious charge. In California, simple kidnapping is defined as moving a person a substantial distance, without the person's consent, by means of force or fear. (California Penal Code 207.) Aggravated kidnapping occurs when, in addition to simple kidnapping, the victim is under 14, ransom is demanded, the victim suffers bodily harm, or the kidnapping is during a carjacking.

"Defenses to kidnapping include consent, that the movement was not a substantial distance, that the evidence is not sufficient, or that the movement consisted of a parent moving his child.

"The penalty for kidnapping, simple or aggravated, consists of incarceration in State prison for a period of years. The penalty could be increased to life WITH the possibility of parole if the kidnapping is for ransom, reward, extortion, or a sex crime.

"The penalty increases to life WITHOUT the possibility of parole if the kidnapping is for ransom, reward, or extortion and the victim suffers death or bodily harm or is placed in a situation that exposes the victim to a substantial likelihood of death.

"Generally, parents cannot be charged with kidnapping their own children unless the taking was with unlawful intent.

"It is interesting to note that in a kidnapping case, unless the victim suffers death or significant bodily harm, the penalties are not as severe as one might think. In my way of thinking, this makes the torture case more interesting, as torture may carry more severe penalties.

"If the prosecution charges a crime which carries a life sentence, particularly a life sentence without the possibility of parole, it might be able to negotiate a plea to a lesser crime. In other words, the specter of a life sentence, particularly a life sentence without the possibility of parole, might make it easier to extract a better plea bargain.

"With respect to you, as to Carbone, on the criminal side, we can allege assault and battery, kidnapping, and torture. On the civil side, we have assault and battery, enhanced by false imprisonment.

"If I were prosecuting this case as a kidnapping, I would make great efforts to prove that the kidnapping included a substantial likelihood of death. Kidnapping with a substantial likelihood of death carries a life sentence without the possibility of parole and places the defendant in much more jeopardy than just a prison sentence which could be reduced.

"As to torture, believe it or not, it is a tough case. Penal Code 206 defines torture as occurring when the defendant inflicts greatly bodily harm and intends to cause cruel or extreme pain for the purpose of revenge, extortion, persuasion, or any sadistic purpose.

"Torture carries a sentence of life with the possibility of parole. Showing great bodily harm with no broken bones might be difficult, but the reason for the harsh sentence is actually the defendant's intent to inflict pain for sadistic purposes, which I think can be shown, particularly with the video evidence.

"I would lean hard on torture. Knowing that the jury will be able to actually see the torture take place coupled with the stiff sentence of life in prison would work to our advantage.

"With respect to Tammy, as to Carbone, I believe that the aggravated kidnapping case is solid. She was under 14. We can't show a sexual component right now, but I think a good case could be made that she was exposed to a substantial likelihood of death, which would up the ante.

"Tammy also has assault and battery charges and false imprisonment claims, both criminal and civil.

"I would submit that the severity and length of her confinement and her treatment might make torture a possibility."

"As to Don, the general rule is that a parent cannot kidnap his or her own child. The prosecution might only charge child abduction. The prosecution might up-grade the charges against Don by claiming that he developed unlawful intent when he allowed Carbone to keep Tammy instead of having him arrested."

Taylor chimed in, "I remember you saying that we would be unable to pursue this case because the police department was bought and paid for by Carbone?"

"That was a consideration; however, since that time I have come up with a different strategy. I plan to go directly to the DA rather than to the police. I know people at the DA's office, and I don't think Carbone was aware that a case could bypass the local police and go directly to the prosecutor."

Taylor responded, "Very good. Learning as we go."

"In speaking with my friends at the DA's office, I was also encouraged to pursue a Department of Justice investigation of the Haven-Newton Police Department, Commissioner Burrows, and Detective Pratt.

"The DOJ prosecutes law enforcement officers for obstruction of justice which includes preventing a victim or witness from reporting misconduct or for writing a false report to conceal misconduct or fabricate evidence. These things were both done in the investigation of Tammy's kidnapping.

"The DA also entertains the claims of victims of real estate fraud. Both Don and Carbone engaged in much fraud with buyers, sellers, and lenders for a couple of years. I plan on having them investigated and their profits disgorged, including the house in

Haven Lakes. The Attorney General might also investigate the mortgage fraud."

The meeting between me and Taylor came to an end.

CHAPTER 41
The Wheels of Justice Turning

The wheels of justice would start to turn; the DA would begin with the criminal indictments for kidnapping, torture, and other sundry crimes against Carbone and others. The DOJ would begin its investigation of the Haven-Newton Police Department, including Burrows and Pratt. The claims of people defrauded by Don and Carbone would be pursued.

Moose's conduct was deemed to be consistent with a citizen's arrest, and no charges were brought against him.

At the time of our meeting at my office, Taylor was reaching the end of her first year at Newton JC. The next year, she transferred to State and then went on to law school.

During the years that she was at State and in law school, the criminal case and fraud investigation against Don and Carbone and the investigation of the Haven-Newton Police Department moved through the Courts along with her civil case against Carbone for assault and battery and false imprisonment.

She was called to give depositions and to testify in court several times, a good learning experience. I too testified, as did Tammy.

Along the way, she settled her civil case against Carbone which gave her enough money to finance law school.

Don, who looked upon himself as a victim, quickly caved in on Carbone and agreed to testify against him in exchange for a lesser sentence. Don agreed to plead guilty to felony child abduction and to serve five years in State prison. He would probably serve three or maybe less.

The DA's investigation into the real estate and loan fraud complaints against Don and Carbone, coupled with attorneys' fees, cost both of them everything they had. Don and his family lost their mansion in Haven Lakes, and Carbone lost his compound. They would both be starting over from scratch when they were released, if they lived that long.

Diane moved back up north with her parents and began teaching at a pre-school. She and Tammy would remain in the Bay Area where Diane's parents had connections and could pitch-in with the child. Fortunately, the boy was a self-starter. He took care of himself and washed his hands of his father. He landed a great job with a tech startup in the Bay Area and moved there to be close to his mother and sister.

Commissioner Burrows was stripped of his commissioner-ship and pension. He would be unable to work for any law enforcement agency or governmental entity in the future. Detective Pratt lost his pension. They were both so pompous when it came to Taylor. They demeaned her every way they could. Their fate was justice at its most sublime. Carbone became the dumping ground for the prosecution. The entire sorry cast of characters including Don, Burrows, Pratt, the entire police department, his guards, and everyone else who knew him fought to be first in line to testify against him.

After all of his protesting and carrying on about his innocence, Carbone pleaded guilty to one count of aggravated kidnapping and one count of torture. He was sentenced to 20 years, which will make him well over 70 when he gets out, that is, if he gets out. He will surely be as hated on the inside as he was on the outside.

There is an old adage which is particularly appropriate here: 'There is no honor among thieves.'

Loyalty, truth, trust, and perseverance won out in the end.

CHAPTER 42

Resolution

Over the past years I stayed with the DA and rose up in the ranks to senior trial deputy. I guess justice was my calling. I met a couple of nice ladies along the way, but I was still so in love with Taylor that I knew that I could never do justice to any other relationship, and I think they knew that too.

I learned that for some of this time, Taylor continued to live with her mother at their farm. I was told that she used some of the money from her lawsuits to improve the farm. I heard that she hired a manager who greatly increased the revenue from the orange operation. I heard that she and the manager expanded the animal raising to include free-range chickens. From them, the farm received numerous awards for what became to be known as the best eggs in the valley.

The expanded operation allowed her to remodel the farm house, and to make a much better living environment for her mother. She and her mother worked hard to settle their differences. Her mother was finally beginning to appreciate all of Taylor's accomplishments and gradually became willing to work with her rather than just against her.

As with most of us, the first year of law school was a shock to Taylor's system. Moving from the ease of undergraduate school to the grind of law school just about pushed her over the edge, particularly when coupled with living with her mother, working a farm, and trying to study.

She finally told her mother that she was going to have to move out and get her own place if she wanted to graduate.

Her mother was surprisingly receptive. She finally appreciated how hard Taylor worked and allowed her to get her own place near campus. Taylor rented a small apartment.

Taylor graduated from law school at the top of her class. Though she had several offers to work at prestigious law firms, she opted for the State Attorney General's Office in nearby Fairfield. Her life too would be dedicated to fighting for justice.

In short order, she became the head of the Attorney General's elder abuse division fighting for the little guy. It suited her for now. I was certain that with her credentials and work ethic she would eventually be moved to the white-collar criminal division in short order.

After I felt that Taylor was sufficiently established in her new life, I somehow worked up the courage to call her. She was so very pleasant, as always, and excited about her new job. She agreed to meet with me. Our plan was to meet at a nice restaurant in Haven. No more Smiley's bar.

I arrived for dinner a little early, as was my custom. I told the hostess that I was waiting for a young lady – sound familiar?

The hostess said that my secret was safe with her.

I was seated at a table from which I see over the dining room to the hostess stand so that I would know when she arrived.

As I was gazing out over the people dining, she walked in.

I was struck.

She was breathtakingly beautiful. It took all of my strength to not gasp for air.

Every person in the room, including the women, turned to look at her. The hostess escorted her to my table. I stood as they approached.

She said, "Do you mind if I sit?"

She sat. We had dinner and talked first at the restaurant and then in her car for hours. We could not get enough of each other. We rehashed the Carbone case. We both decided that loyalty, truth, and dedication were the real winners.

When things got a little tough, Carbone's cronies cut and ran, leaving him holding the bag for everyone. She, on the other hand, hung in through thick and thin to find Tammy and bring her home, regardless of personal sacrifice.

Over the next months we met regularly. It started out as friendship, which was her way as she was still a little uneasy with men. Eventually, trust was built, and we became lovers.

I spent entirely too much on a truly beautiful diamond ring. We met for dinner at our favorite restaurant. After dinner, next to our table, I got down on one knee and proposed.

The time between my proposal and her speaking seemed to be an eternity. I was shaking. After a long silence, I was waiting for the verdict.

She finally looked at me and replied: "Yes."

And so began our most beautiful life together.